"You had a nanny growing up?" He sounded surprised.

"Yes, I did. My mother died when I was a baby, and my father's job was very demanding."

"You miss her." It wasn't a question. He sounded as if he understood.

"I do. I wish I could have her with me and take care of her—the way she took care of me."

"I know what you mean." One side of his mouth tipped up in a smile. "For me, it's my foster mom, Ruby. She took care of me when nobody else would. The people who love us when nobody else does, when we're the most unlovable, those are the people you never forget." His jaw firmed up. "I want to give that to the boys, if I can."

Oh, she was sunk.

"I only have the summer," she heard herself saying. "When the Shermans get back from Europe, they expect me to come back to work for them."

"Understood. So? Do we have ourselves a deal?"

She hesitated, although she already knew what she was going to say. "We have a deal."

Laurel Blount lives on a small farm in Georgia with her husband, David, their four children, a milk cow, dairy goats, assorted chickens, an enormous dog, three spoiled cats and one extremely bossy goose with boundary issues. She divides her time between farm chores, homeschooling and writing, and she's happiest with a cup of steaming tea at her elbow and a good book in her hand.

Books by Laurel Blount

Love Inspired

A Family for the Farmer
A Baby for the Minister
Hometown Hope
A Rancher to Trust
Lost and Found Faith
Her Mountain Refuge
Together for the Twins

Visit the Author Profile page at LoveInspired.com.

Together
for the Twins

Laurel Blount

LOVE INSPIRED
INSPIRATIONAL ROMANCE

LOVE INSPIRED®
INSPIRATIONAL ROMANCE

Recycling programs for this product may not exist in your area.

ISBN-13: 978-1-335-58630-8

Together for the Twins

For questions and comments about the quality of this book, please contact us at CustomerService@Harlequin.com.

Love Inspired
22 Adelaide St. West, 41st Floor
Toronto, Ontario M5H 4E3, Canada
www.LoveInspired.com

Printed in U.S.A.

Bear ye one another's burdens,
and so fulfil the law of Christ.
—*Galatians* 6:2

For my brother-in-law Shawn Hall,
salesman extraordinaire and bighearted
adoptive dad, who graciously provided insights
on the dynamics of his profession.

Chapter One

Lunch at Burger Burger had been a disaster, and the drive back to the Cedar Ridge Public Library wasn't going much better.

No surprise there, Ryder Montgomery thought grimly. These days his life was just one catastrophe after another.

He glanced in the rearview mirror at his twin four-year-old nephews, strapped in their brand-new car seats. It had taken him fifteen minutes and six miniature chocolate bars to get them in those seats, but he'd managed it.

Barely.

Like everything else involving the twins, car seats were a battle. So were baths, toothbrushing—and meals, as the yellow mustard stain running up his shirtsleeve reminded him. A food flinging fit had broken out when the boys had been served chicken nuggets instead of macaroni and cheese. Pasta out of a rectangular blue box had been the only twin-approved lunch since he'd taken charge of them three weeks ago in mid-May.

Or, more accurately, since they'd taken charge of him.

There was no use sugarcoating it. He was flunking this instant dad thing, big-time. It didn't help that the twins had no fear and were what his foster mom, Ruby, called muleheaded—a dangerous combo. He'd already made not one but two terrifying trips to the local ER with a screaming child—experiences that had surely lopped a decade off his life expectancy.

Those had turned out all right, but his nerves couldn't take any more near misses. He was trying his best to keep them safe, but these kids paid zero attention to him—or any other adult. They were unpredictable, accident-prone and bursting with energy.

They also had an endless repertoire of annoying noises. Like now—Benji had been making an off-key screeching noise ever since they pulled out of the hamburger joint's parking lot. It was making Ryder's ears ring. Apparently Benji's twin, Tucker, didn't like it much better.

"Stop that," Tucker demanded.

Benji's screeching went up a couple of decibels. Uh-oh. Ryder's fingers tensed around the steering wheel. Most of the time, these two kids battled as a team, which was bad enough. But when they turned on each other? Then things got ugly fast, and he was one more hair-raising experience away from a stroke.

He mentally calculated how far they were from the library. His sister-in-law was there waiting to help him out with this nanny interview. Maybe between the two of them, they could get the boys under control.

Maybe. But he had to make it there first.

"Getting a little loud back there," he said in a *let's all be friends* kind of tone. "Dial it down a few notches, Benji, okay?"

The screeching only grew shriller.

Tucker made an exasperated noise. "I told you to stop it!"

Ryder shot another glance in the mirror just in time to see the little boy wrench off his blue tennis shoe and fling it at his brother.

Pow. Straight hit to the nose. In spite of everything, Ryder's ex-baseball-pitcher mind stood up and applauded. The kid had an arm.

Then the screaming started, and Ryder groaned and rubbed at his forehead.

He wanted out of this car.

He wanted out of this whole situation.

Up until three weeks ago, his life had been going according to plan. He'd left his job with

Atlanta Media and opened his start-up business as a sales consultant right on schedule, with a decent roster of clients who wanted him to coach their sales teams to higher numbers. That was all well and good, but if he couldn't get back to work soon, his bank balance was going to take a serious beating.

That possibility scared him to death because money mattered—a lot. His dad's gambling addiction had taught Ryder that before he'd turned ten.

That and a set of survival skills like dumpster diving and how to make tomato soup out of ketchup packets swiped from the local diner.

He'd retired those skills after the foster care system had placed him at Ruby Sawyer's farm. Ruby never had much money either, but she made sure the kids under her roof never went without a single thing they needed. The first night there, Ryder had gone to bed with a full stomach for the first time in months. He was fourteen years old at the time, but he'd pressed his face into his freshly washed pillowcase and cried like a baby out of sheer relief.

Ruby and his five foster siblings, Logan, Maggie, Torey, Nick and Jina had been Ryder's family ever since, and his mission in life was to make enough money so these people he loved never went without anything they needed. Thanks to some finely honed salesman skills, he'd been well on his way to that goal—until a middle-of-the-night phone call from Colorado forced him to put his fledgling business on hold and move home to Cedar Ridge, Georgia.

Where he was now being held hostage by two tiny terrorists.

A second small shoe sailed past his head and bounced off the rearview mirror. He pressed down harder on the accelerator, remembering that his passport was still in the glove compartment from a business trip he'd taken to Canada a month ago.

For a second, he entertained the fantasy of leaving the twins at the library and hopping a plane to someplace tropical. He'd change his name and set up some kind of business. A surf shop maybe.

He knew almost nothing about surfing—but that was still more than he knew about four-year-olds. His sister had made a lot of not-so-smart decisions in her short, troubled life, but leaving a clueless bachelor like him in charge of her boys topped the list.

He swung into the library lot and parked beside Logan's patrol car just as Benji managed to unbuckle his straps. The brown-haired twin launched himself across the back seat at his tow-headed brother, biting and scratching.

"Whoa, whoa, *whoa*!" Ryder scrambled to get out of the car. He yanked open the back door and reached in, pulling the two kids apart. They strained toward each other, swinging and spitting, like two feral cats. "Calm down, guys!"

It made no difference. Nothing he said ever did.

"Having some trouble?"

Logan was heading in their direction. The sheriff's expression was a mixture of concern and alarm—but not surprise. Nobody in his family was surprised by the twins' misbehavior anymore.

"Give me a hand, will you?"

Logan took charge of Benji. "Settle down," he said in a tone that had put dozens of juvenile delinquents in their places.

It didn't have much effect on Benji.

Ryder picked Tucker up and fished around in the car until he located the two sneakers. He sat the boy on the edge of the back seat and began cramming the shoes back on the struggling preschooler's feet.

"Where's Charlotte?" Ryder asked. His sister-in-law had promised to supervise the boys during the library's story hour so that he could get this nanny interview done in relative peace.

"In the library trying to sweet-talk the children's librarian into letting these two back inside.

Apparently they're on some kind of library no-fly list. What happened here last week, Ryder?"

He winced. "There was a book-throwing incident."

"Incident?" Logan lifted an eyebrow.

His brother could sniff out a half truth like a bloodhound. "One of the books hit the children's librarian right in the eye," Ryder admitted.

Logan shook his head slowly. "Ryder—"

"I know. Okay? I'm working on it." He was relieved to see Charlotte heading their way—until he noticed her expression.

Uh-oh.

"There's been a change of plans," she announced when she was within earshot, pitching her voice to be heard over the boys' fussing. "Mrs. Bishop won't budge. The twins are banned from the library until further notice."

Oh, brother. "I'll go talk to her."

"No." Charlotte shook her head. "I wouldn't, Ryder. Even your legendary charm isn't likely to work today. She's completely out of patience." She didn't add *like the rest of us*, but he heard the words anyway. His sister-in-law squared her shoulders. "It's a nice day. I'll take the boys to the puppy park while you do the interview."

The boys stopped squabbling and turned their heads in her direction.

"Puppy park?" Benji repeated. He shared a

long look with his brother, and Ryder's skin prickled.

That look always meant trouble.

"You sure that's a good idea?" Logan was asking his wife.

"It's the only idea we've got," she replied shortly. "And it's the only way Ryder can interview the nanny—who, I sincerely hope and pray, turns out to be a perfect fit for this job. Come on, guys." She tried to take the twins' hands, but they evaded her grasp, skipping down the sidewalk. She hurried after them. "Boys! Slow down! Wait for me!"

Ryder watched her go with a feeling of impending doom. Logan must have felt the same way, because his brother cut him a narrow glance.

"I'm fond of my wife, Ryder," Logan said ominously. "She gets hurt, I'm going to be upset."

"Me, too." Ryder rubbed his jaw. Maybe this was as good a time as any to bring up the idea he'd been kicking around since that trip to the emergency room when the pediatrician had plucked a LEGO from Tucker's nose. "Look, Logan. It may not look like it, but I'm doing my best. Parenting obviously isn't my strong point. Maybe I should give up custody of the boys to you and Charlotte, or to Neil and Maggie. You guys know how to raise kids. I don't. I'd contribute financially and could be a part of their lives, but—"

"Hold on." Logan looked alarmed. "I think you're jumping the gun. Nobody knows how to parent right out of the gate, and you got thrown into the deep end with these two. You'll figure it out. Give yourself time."

"What if I don't? You and I both know first-hand what it's like to grow up without a decent dad. I'd hate for that to happen to the twins."

"You're doing better than you think you are. Look, if things don't get better in a few months, then we'll talk again, okay? We'll figure something out together. Tucker and Benji are part of our family now, and between the five of us and Ruby, we'll find a way to help them. You're not alone in this. All right?"

"Thanks." The simple word didn't seem like nearly enough, but it was the best he could manage.

His brother shrugged. "It's what we do, Ryder. We help each other. You know that." He glanced at his watch. "I've got to get back to the office. I came by to tell you that the nanny's background check came back squeaky-clean. The woman doesn't have so much as a parking ticket."

"Good."

"Very good. Because you need to hire some

professional help, bro. Like I said just now, we're all behind you, but the twins are hard to handle."

"Hard's an understatement."

"I wish I could help more, but my job's keeping me hopping these days."

"I understand. And you and Maggie have your own families to see to. Plus, Maggie's got the bakery to run." Their foster sister was co-owner of Angelo's, a local eatery. "And Ruby…"

"Yeah." Logan frowned. "Ruby's another issue. You and the boys living on the farm with her—I don't want to hurt your feelings, and she'd kill me for saying anything, but—"

Ryder knew where this was going. He'd been thinking the same thing. "It's not working out."

"No, it's not. I know you moved back in so she could help with the twins. She loved the idea, but Ruby's not as young as she used to be, and these dizzy spells she keeps having…" Logan shook his head. "I'm worried about her. We all are."

"I'm worried too. I'll find someplace to rent in town."

"I think that's a good idea. Better put your salesman skills to good use and get this nanny on board. If you're on your own, you're really going to need the help."

"You're right about that."

His brother clapped him on the back. "We'll figure this out." As he got into his patrol car,

Logan shot him a look that was a mixture of tease and threat. "I meant what I said about Charlotte, though. I want my wife back in one piece."

After Logan pulled out of the parking lot, Ryder headed inside, avoiding the reproachful gaze of Mrs. Bishop, who'd been the children's librarian as long as he could remember. He took a table by the door where he could see when the nanny applicant came in.

Although, come to think of it, he wasn't sure how he'd recognize her. The hurried emails they'd exchanged setting up the meet hadn't included a photo. Quickly he took out his phone and tapped a message to his computer geek sister, Torey.

Ten minutes later, his phone chirped, earning another harsh look from Mrs. Bishop.

Torey had sent a picture. Meet Elise Cooper, the caption said.

A young woman looked out of the screen at him, her eyebrows arched. Good-looking, he decided, in an understated way. She wasn't magazine-pretty, but she had a face that made you look twice. Maybe it was the eyes—wide and sweetly serious. He used his fingers to enlarge the photo, and leaned in close, trying to discern what color they were. Hazel, maybe?

Before he could decide, the door to the library banged open. Charlotte staggered in.

"Ryder!" She leaned against the door and beckoned to him, apparently too breathless to speak.

Uh-oh. He rose, shoving the phone into his pocket. "What happened?"

Something bad. With the twins it was always something bad.

"Shhhh!" the librarian fussed, but Ryder paid no attention. He'd noticed something else.

Charlotte's hand was bleeding.

"Are you all right?" He snagged a couple of tissues off the circulation desk as he passed it and inspected her hand. "Did something *bite* you?" Oh, no. "Is it serious? Charlotte, did one of the boys—"

Logan was going to kill him.

"No, not the boys. Dog." His sister-in-law was still struggling to catch her breath. "They chased this Chihuahua—" She stopped and shook her head. "Long story. She had a rabies tag, so it's okay. Come on." She tugged at his hand. "The boys are out front, and you've got to see—"

The boys. If Charlotte was in here, who was watching the boys?

"Oh, no." No telling what trouble those two would get into while they were unsupervised. They got into plenty of it when they *were* supervised. He brushed swiftly past her, heading for the door.

"They're fine!" she called after him. "You'll see!"

He pushed out into the bright sunlight. "Benji? Tucker!"

"Over here." The answering voice was calm and held the faintest hint of a British accent.

He turned. The twins were seated on a concrete bench under a large magnolia tree. Between them sat the woman from the picture. She looked different—her hair was down, held away from her face by a band and tumbling to her shoulders. She wore a slim-fitting gray suit and a dark pink blouse.

Benji and Tucker sat beside her, feet swinging back and forth. Their faces were dirty, and Tucker's collar was ripped halfway off, but they seemed oddly calm.

The woman rose, tugging her jacket neatly into place. "Wait here, please," she instructed the boys. She walked toward him, and the twins stayed on the bench.

They *stayed*.

Ryder stared, his mind struggling to make sense of what he was seeing.

She'd told them to wait, and they *had*. When he told them to wait, they usually took off in two different directions at full speed.

The woman cleared her throat, and he pulled his eyes away from the twins. She stood in front of him, one hand politely extended.

"Elise Cooper," she said. "And you must be Ryder Montgomery. I believe we have an interview scheduled."

She said *scheduled* the way the Brits did, with the *sh* sound. And her eyes turned out to be a pretty mixture of green and brown.

"Forget the interview." He took her hand and shook it firmly. "You're hired."

Hired? Already? Was he serious?

Elise blinked at the handsome, dark-haired man who was shaking her hand so enthusiastically that her bracelets rattled.

He certainly seemed serious.

He was in his early thirties, she'd guess, with a strong face that was saved from perfection by a nose that had been broken at some time or other. He had a level way of looking her in the eye that she liked—and a take-no-prisoners energy that sent up a warning flare.

Her father had that kind of focused drive, too, and she'd learned to distrust it. Maybe it was an asset in the boardroom, but when he used it to bulldoze his daughter, it caused serious problems.

Like now, for instance. She wouldn't even be here interviewing for this stopgap job if it weren't for her father's underhanded scheming.

Well, for once Andrew Cooper wasn't getting his way. She straightened her shoulders and pulled her hand free.

"Mr. Montgomery—" she began.

"Ryder. Please." He smiled, and a lone dimple twinkled in his left cheek. Just the one—which gave him a lopsided boyish charm. Quite appealing, actually.

Elise frowned and scolded herself. This man's dimple was none of her business.

"Ryder," she repeated. "I'm happy I've made a good first impression."

"That's an understatement." He nodded at the boys. "Look at them. They're just *sitting* there."

She looked. "And?"

"And they're doing what you told them to do."

She looked again. "More or less." They were squirming, and their foot swinging had ramped up. She gave it five minutes before they were into some sort of mischief.

Maybe less. She smiled.

She did appreciate a challenge.

"More or less is a major improvement," their uncle was saying. "I'm serious. If you want this job, it's yours."

"Well, that's very good to hear."

She didn't want this job. She needed this job. Otherwise her father was going to get his way and drag her back to his house in Charleston for the summer, and that, she was absolutely determined, was not going to happen.

Not this time. Not after he'd pulled strings to get her not only unemployed but homeless for three solid months. All so he could have the opportunity to fling yet another series of ambitious young executives at her, all anxious to date the CEO's daughter and put themselves on the fast track to a promotion.

This time her father had gone too far. He'd interfered with her job—her livelihood. This was a new low, even for him.

"I'm very interested in this job." Elise lifted her chin a notch. "But before we firm up our arrangement, we should probably sit down with your wife, don't you think? And discuss all the details?"

She should have asked more questions ahead of time. But when her employers, the Shermans, had offhandedly mentioned that a friend of a friend was looking for a nanny for the summer, she'd jumped on it. Thanks to her scoundrel of a father finagling a working three-month vacation for Jon Sherman—in Paris, no less, with childcare conveniently provided —she couldn't afford to be picky. Ryder Montgomery had been an answer to her prayers.

Right now her answer-to-prayer was looking at her oddly. "My wife? Come to think of it, we probably do need to go over a few details. Why don't we—"

Before he could finish his sentence, a siren wailed behind them, and a sheriff's car pulled up to the curb, lights flashing. A broad-shouldered officer jumped out and strode up the sidewalk.

"Here we go," Ryder muttered.

"What's going on?"

He sighed. "Let's just say news travels fast in small towns."

"One piece." The sheriff bit out as he got closer. "One piece, I said. If you weren't my brother, I'd—"

The door to the library banged open, and the woman she'd helped in the parking lot—the one she assumed was Ryder's wife—hurried down the steps. She had a wad of tissues clamped around her wounded finger, and she looked annoyed. "Logan, leave Ryder alone. I'm fine!"

"You're not fine. You're bleeding." The sheriff shouldered past them and went to her. "Animal bites can be nasty." He gently unwrapped the tissue from her finger. "I'll drive you over to the fire station. They'll have all the first aid stuff there, and I'll get one of the paramedics to look at it. He'll know if you need to go to the emergency room."

"Oh, for pity's sake. Being nipped by a Chihuahua doesn't constitute a medical emergency.

I'm sorry I texted you. I thought you'd think it was funny. The dog was the size of my shoe and wearing a pink sweater. Ryder, talk some sense into your brother, would you?"

"Can't help you," Ryder said dryly. "Talking sense into Logan's hard head is outside of my skill set. Particularly where you're concerned." He turned to Elise. "Would you excuse me just a second?"

"Of course." She caught movement out of the corner of her eye and turned her head just in time to see one twin—Tucker, she believed his name was—give his brother a shove.

"Benji and Tucker, come here, please." She issued the command in her nanny voice. Firm, pleasant—and non-negotiable.

The boys froze, each with a fistful of the other's shirt. She watched them think it over, glancing at each other, then back to her, trying to decide if they were going to do what she said or not.

She arched one eyebrow.

That did it. As she'd hoped, she was still enough of an unknown that they weren't quite sure how far to push her. They got up and trudged in her direction.

"Why don't we go into the library and choose a book?" Maybe that would keep them occupied for a few moments.

"Can't," Tucker said.

"Why not?"

"'Cause we can't go in the library no more," Benji explained.

"Anymore." Elise made the correction automatically. "And why is that?"

The two exchanged a glance. "We hit the lady librarian with a book, but we didn't mean to. We was trying to chunk it in the trash can, and she was standing next to it."

"I see." This time both of Elise's eyebrows went up. "And why were you trying to throw a library book into the trash can?"

Tucker shrugged. "Them books was boring. So we tore them up and throwed them."

Both of the boys looked up at her defiantly, not a smidge of remorse on their faces.

Oh, yes. Plenty of work to do here. These two little rascals needed her desperately.

She glanced up to find Ryder walking in her direction as the sheriff led the still-protesting blonde woman to his patrol car.

"Sorry about that," he said. "My brother can be a little overprotective. He's taking my sister-in-law to get that bite checked out."

"Your sister-in-law?" Her heart sank. Well, the situation with the overprotective sheriff certainly made more sense now. "The boys called her Aunt Charlotte, and I assumed—"

"That she was my wife. Understandable mistake, but no. I'm not married." He frowned, scanning her face. "Is that going to be a problem?"

She was tempted to say no. She really needed this job.

On the other hand, that one rather spectacular—and humiliating—episode six years ago was quite enough, thank you very much. She'd set this particular rule for a very good reason, and she wasn't going to bend it. Not even to checkmate her father.

"I'm terribly sorry," she said. "But yes. I'm afraid it is."

Chapter Two

Ryder's relief went straight into a nosedive, but he forced himself not to panic.

He'd had deals go south before—it happened in sales all the time. Desperation never helped.

The trouble was, he felt desperate. He needed Elise Cooper to take this job. The woman was amazing. She'd only been around the boys for fifteen minutes, and already they were behaving better than they ever had for him.

"Could I ask why?"

"I don't accept positions with single fathers. It's nothing personal. It's just a…policy of mine."

Her answer was straightforward enough, but pain flickered across her face as she gave it. Just one little wince, but he'd learned to pay attention to things like that. A good salesman always did.

People's faces told you more than their words ever did.

This not-personal policy had a painful history attached to it. He'd grown up around girls, first his half-sister Carrie, and then his three foster sisters, so he could guess what had happened. Some guy had been a jerk. He tightened his jaw.

"Whatever happened that made you set this policy up, I guarantee it won't be a problem in this case. You have my word. I can provide character references, too, if that would help."

She was shaking her head before he'd finished the sentence. "I'm sorry. It's my understanding that this is a live-in position, and it's just rather—awkward under those circumstances."

Her cheeks were pink. This discussion was making her uncomfortable, and that wasn't good. If she shut this conversation down now, he'd never get the chance to convince her he wasn't like Jerk Guy.

First rules of sales: keep 'em talking.

"What if it wasn't live-in? Would that work?"

Her delicate brows drew together as she studied him. She was considering it. Good.

"That would cause a different issue. Room and board are generally included in the job. I can't afford to finance my own housing costs out of my salary."

Ryder picked up a subtle questioning inflection in Elise's voice. She still wasn't on board, but she'd pitched the ball back into his court.

The knot in the pit of his stomach loosened, and he sent up a thankful prayer.

He was back in the game.

"That sounds like something we could figure out."

She lifted an eyebrow. "If you have to pay for separate living quarters for me, that will ramp up your costs quite a bit. Are you willing to do that?"

Yes, he was. However, he didn't have a lot of extra money to throw around right now. Starting his new business had done some damage to his emergency fund, and since he'd be leaving Ruby's, he also had to finance housing for himself and the twins.

He needed to buy some time while he thought this through. "I'm sure we can work something out. In the meantime, why don't we go ahead with the interview?" When she hesitated, he nudged, "You've already come all this way. What do you have to lose?"

She thought it over. "Very well. But where are we going to have this interview? I hear the library is currently off-limits." She glanced at the boys and tsked her tongue. "Such a pity. When you find the right books—and they're there, hidden like Easter eggs among the boring ones—libraries are full of wonderful adventures. Pirates and dinosaurs. Monsters and trains." She sighed sadly. "Such a shame."

Ryder watched the twins' faces as Elise outlined the joys of reading. He saw a spark of genuine interest—and something else. He wasn't sure, but it might—just possibly—have been regret.

That was a first. The boys were never sorry for anything they did. Ever. In fact, that was one of the things that worried him most about them.

Their mom, his half sister, had been the same way—impulsive, defiant. Stubborn. It hadn't ended well. He hadn't heard from Carrie in five years—not since she'd walked out of the last rehab center he'd pulled strings to get her into. He hadn't even known about the boys. The Denver police officer who'd notified him of her death said she'd suffered a heart attack brought on by a decade of substance abuse.

That news had stomped his heart flat.

He didn't want the twins following in their mom's footsteps, and he was going to do everything he could to prevent it. Starting now. He and the boys needed this woman's help. He just had to hash out a deal she felt comfortable with.

The good news was, this was something he actually had a shot at pulling off. His fatherhood skills might be entry-level, but dealmaking?

That was his bread and butter.

He thought fast, sifting through their options. Probably better avoid the puppy park. He'd al-

ready had one babysitter benched by a Chihuahua bite.

"We could drive to Angelo's and talk," he suggested. "My foster sister Maggie's half owner,
and the boys love the cookies she bakes. It's just
down at the end of the street. In fact, you can see
it from here." Maybe Maggie's cookies would
keep the boys busy long enough for them to talk.

Probably not, but a guy could hope.

She shaded her eyes with one hand and looked
where he was pointing. "That place with the
striped awnings? Why on earth would we drive?
It's an easy walk."

Easy walk. Ryder almost laughed out loud.
Yeah, right.

"The twins aren't exactly…trustworthy about
staying on sidewalks, and they don't like to hold
hands." In fact, they point blank refused to hold
hands, throwing epic fits when a grown-up insisted. He had the bruises on his shins to prove it.

Elise didn't bat an eyelash. "I'm sure that won't
be a problem." She leaned down so she was on
eye level with the twins. "All right, boys, how
shall we walk? We'll need to hold hands when
we cross the street, of course, but do you need to
hold a grown-up's hand to remember to stay on
the sidewalk? Or are you old enough to do that
by yourselves without my help?"

Benji and Tucker seemed surprised by the

choice. They looked at each other, and then back at Elise.

"By ourselves," they said together.

She nodded. "Fine." She straightened and backed up about five feet. "See how far apart we are now?"

The boys nodded.

"That's as far apart as we ever need to be." She tilted her head. "Any farther than that, and we'll have to go back to holding hands all the time." She pursed her lips, looking thoughtful. "That may be tricky to remember. I know! We'll pretend there's an invisible rope between us and it only stretches that far. Will you be able to do that?"

"Yeah," Benji said quickly. Tucker nodded his agreement, too.

Ryder watched this interchange with a sense of awe. The twins were *listening*.

"Wonderful." Approval purred warmly in her voice. "You're both quite smart, aren't you?" She clapped her hands briskly. "Off you go! Remember that invisible rope!"

"Okay!" Tucker assured her. This time it was Benji's turn to nod. The boys scampered down the sidewalk, right to the end of Elise's imaginary boundary.

And—of course—they kept right on going.

Just as his heart sank, Elise cleared her throat. Such a small, ordinary noise, but it did the job.

e, okay? He'd done that once, out of pure
ation.
d he?" Elise appeared unmoved by this
ttering revelation. "Probably that day he
oo tired to make good choices himself. It
ens to grown-ups sometimes, just like little
. He won't do that today. Not with me here."
inhaled. "Mmm. I smell something good.
't you? Must be some fresh goodies coming
of the oven. Do you know that in England
y call cookies biscuits?"
The boys' eyes widened.
"Cookies ain't *biscuits*," Tucker informed her
a disgusted tone. "Biscuits is what you put but-

The boys stopped short and glanced back, measuring the distance between themselves and the two adults. Then, to his amazement, they backed up three steps and walked on at a normal pace.

Ryder stared at his nephews in stupefied disbelief before turning his wondering gaze back to Elise. Who *was* she? Some sort of kid-whispering nanny ninja?

He had to hire this woman.

"How did you *do* that? I can't even get them to brush their teeth. Granted, I'm a clueless rookie, but it's not just me. Nobody in my family can get them to cooperate, not even Ruby."

"Ruby?"

"My foster mom. She brought six of us up— and we weren't the easiest kids. That's why I came back home to stay with her. I figured if anybody could teach me the ropes, she could. But she's getting older…" Wow, it hurt to say that. "And the twins are too much for her. It's gotten so bad that I'm looking for a house to rent, just to give Ruby a break. But today you show up and…" He gestured to the boys walking in front of them. "They start acting like *that*. I'm not usually at a loss for words, believe me. But I am right now. You're incredible."

She tilted her head, as if deflecting the compliment. "That's very kind, but don't get too excited. They don't know me well yet. If we spend much time together, they'll test me. Children always do."

"But you'd pass that test. Wouldn't you?"

She shrugged, but her eyes twinkled. "I generally do."

He believed her.

They'd reached Angelo's. The little bakery was directly across the street, and the enticing smells of warm cookies and baking bread filled the air. Elise stepped to the curb and calmly offered a hand to each twin. They ignored her, and Ryder's gut tensed.

Showtime.

Life with the twins was like walking through a minefield. One wrong step—and boom. A big, loud, messy ordeal.

He had to admit, he was interested to see how Elise would handle this.

"Boys." Her voice was pleasant—and firm. "Hands, please, just while we cross the street."

The twins looked at each other, and the knot in Ryder's stomach tightened. Nope, this wasn't going to go well.

"We ain't holding nobody's hands. We ain't babies," Tucker announced.

Elise lifted a brow. "No, you *aren't* babies," she agreed, stressing the correction. "So the decision is entirely up to you." The boys' expres-

sions brightened—until she add want cookies, we'll continue wal of the street."

"Uh-uh. We do want cookies,"

"I'm glad to hear it. I do, too." She and kept her hands out. "But if you hands to cross the street, nobody wil

The twins' expressions darkened.

"We'll pitch a fit," Benji promised g

"Guys—" Ryder started. Elise sho quelling look and gave the tiniest shake head.

Let me handle this.

He held up his hands in silent surrender.
Knock yourself out

as Benji took her other hand. "They're quite interesting, bees. Much smarter than you'd think, really. Do you know—"

She kept talking as she walked with the boys across the street, but Ryder wasn't listening. He couldn't have cared less about bees or biscuits.

The only thing he cared about right now was Elise Cooper.

He had to convince this woman to take the job. Period, end of story. Whatever it took.

Maybe he hadn't seen much good parenting before coming to Ruby's house as a teenager, but he'd seen plenty since. Ruby, of course, was a genius with kids. His foster sister Maggie was a great mom to her growing brood, and Logan and Charlotte were awesome parents, too.

And Elise Cooper left them all in the dust, at least where the twins were concerned.

He tried to think of some way he could sweeten the deal for her. He couldn't up the salary offer much, and he wasn't sure that would do the trick anyway.

Some people lived and died by their bank balances—and some people didn't. Going by the quiet, understated way Elise dressed and the level, honest way she looked at him, he suspected she fell into the second category. He'd have to figure out some other way to—

Honk!

He jumped, and discovered he was standing four inches away from the hood of a vintage Mercedes. Mabel Winston poked her freshly permed gray head out the car window and glared at him.

"Ryder Montgomery, you scared me out of my wits! I almost ran you over!"

"Sorry, Mrs. Mabel. I wasn't watching where I was going." He jogged across the street to where Elise and the twins waited on the sidewalk in front of Angelo's.

Mabel shook her finger at him. "You better start watching, for both our sakes! Sheriff Logan's already said if I mow down one more mailbox, he's taking my license away. Just imagine what he'd do if I flattened his brother! I wouldn't ever get to drive again, and then how will I get my hair done for church? Tell me that!" Before he came up with an answer, she pulled her head back in the window and gunned the old car's motor, roaring past him.

Elise and the boys considered him, wide-eyed.

"Maybe Uncle Ryder better hold somebody's hand on the way back," Tucker suggested solemnly.

Elise's mouth twitched as her eyes met Ryder's. "Good idea. Now, come along, boys. Let's go see about those cookies!"

Ushering the boys ahead of her, she herded them inside the bakery.

* * *

Elise fell in love with Angelo's at first sniff. It smelled like cozy comfort, a delightful mix of coffee, cinnamon and hot sugar. The place was small, but bright and spotlessly clean.

A balding, heavyset man in a white apron was adding fresh pastries to a glass display counter. He gave the twins an alarmed look and carefully scooted a few breakable items out of a child's reach on the counter.

Elise smothered a smile. Apparently, he'd met the boys before.

Ryder seemed to be pretty well-known, too. As they made their way to a vacant table, several customers greeted him by name—in a much nicer tone than that scolding woman driving the sedan. Elise's smile widened at the memory.

It wasn't funny, she scolded herself sternly. He could have been hurt.

But he hadn't been—and it had been a little funny.

"Be there in a minute!" A red-haired woman working at the counter waved at them. Probably Ryder's sister, Elise guessed.

She and Ryder settled themselves and the boys at a table. With a bit of subtle finagling, Elise managed to herd the twins into the chairs next to the window overlooking the street, which hopefully would keep them both entertained and safely corralled.

Elise liked the view herself, and she'd enjoyed the short walk. Cedar Ridge was a pretty place. She appreciated the old-fashioned feel of the weathered brick store buildings—each housing a mom-and-pop style business—and the wide, litter-free streets. She could see the steeple of a church in the distance, set against the backdrop of the surrounding Blue Ridge Mountains.

Those steep hills had given her a moment or two of nerves when she'd driven up their winding slopes, but from here, they lent a sense of protection and peace. They seemed to be sheltering this sweet town, keeping the hectic modern world at arm's length.

She'd never spent much time in small towns. Her ambitious father had always craved the hustle and the opportunities of cities, and people who needed nannies tended to live in areas with higher-income job opportunities.

But she'd read stories about small-town life, and she'd listened to Nanny Bev's tales of growing up in a village in England. It might be nice to spend a summer here—if things could be worked out.

She glanced at Ryder, who was quietly moving their napkin dispensers and salt and pepper shakers to the vacant table behind them. He seemed pleasant enough and polite, and there was certainly no doubt he needed her help with the boys.

If only he were older or married—or not quite so good-looking.

"Brace yourself," Ryder murmured. She glanced at him, startled out of her thoughts.

"What?"

"You're about to meet my sister, and she's a force to be reckoned with."

"Hi!" The ruddy-haired woman hurried to their table, beaming with bright interest. "You must be the nanny." She extended a hand, which Elise accepted. "Elise, right? I'm Maggie, Ryder's sister. I can't tell you how great it is to meet you. Charlotte tells me you're like a modern Mary Poppins."

"She's very kind. How is she, by the way?"

"Aggravated with Logan," Maggie said with a chuckle. "Other than that, she's fine. No stitches, just a newfound respect for tiny dogs wearing sweaters." The other woman reached over and flicked Tucker's torn collar. "Speaking of clothes, looks like you're going to have to do some shopping, Uncle Ryder. These boys are starting to look like ragamuffins. Okay, kiddos, I just took a tray of double chocolate chip cookies out of the oven. I'll bring you each one and some milk. Ryder, what will you have?"

"Just coffee."

"Leaded or unleaded?"

"Leaded. I need the caffeine. I'm not getting much sleep these days."

Maggie winked at Elise. "Hopefully that's going to change now. Elise, what would you—"

"I got to go," Benji interrupted. Ryder's expression changed to one of alarm, and he jumped up as if he'd been jabbed with a stick.

"Come on, then," he said. "Tucker, why don't you come, too? Their bladders are in perfect sync," he explained to Elise. "When one has to go, the other one almost always does too."

"And we don't want any more accidents." Maggie cut a wary glance behind herself at the door leading into the kitchen. "Angelo still hasn't recovered from that last one."

Benji was shifting his weight from one foot to the other, while Tucker leaned back in his chair looking as if he were thinking the whole thing over.

"Hurry, up, Tuck," Ryder said uneasily, watching Benji's uncomfortable dancing.

"Go ahead. You'll need to wash your hands before you can have the cookies," Elise said pleasantly. "Of course, if you'd rather, I can take you into the ladies' washroom while—"

"No!" Tucker looked appalled. "I ain't no lady!"

"Very well," Elise said easily. "Go ahead with your uncle, then, if you'd rather." Tucker rose and started across the café with his brother and uncle.

Maggie dropped into the chair Ryder had vacated. "Charlotte was right," she said. "You really are amazing. Last Wednesday morning,

Tucker wouldn't go with Benji, and he ended up having an accident right in front of the women's Bible and Bagels study group. Angelo mopped the floor five times with bleach, and he still hides in the kitchen when he sees them coming. But you just—" She shook her head. "I don't even know what you did just now, but it sure worked!" To Elise's surprise, Maggie reached over and squeezed her hand. "You're an answer to our prayers, Elise Cooper. My brother's a good guy, and he's trying really hard, but he's barely keeping his head above water."

Elise glanced toward the restroom area. Ryder and the boys hadn't reappeared yet. "How long has he had guardianship of the twins?"

"Three weeks," Maggie said. "His sister Carrie—the boys' mom—died unexpectedly."

"I'm so sorry. I'm an only child, but I'm sure that's a very hard loss."

"I can't imagine losing one of my brothers or sisters," Maggie agreed. "Of course, we're all fosters, so not biologically related, but that's never made any difference. The six of us are really close. Carrie was Ryder's half sister, and she stayed with his stepmom after the divorce, so they never spent a lot of time together."

"But she left him custody of her sons?" That seemed odd.

"Well, sure." Maggie didn't seem to think that

was remarkable at all. "She knew he'd take care of them. And he will. Not that this whole thing hasn't knocked him for a loop. Ryder's always been laser-focused on his career. Kids have never been on his radar. Plus the boys are…" Maggie paused, apparently searching for a polite word.

"Challenging," Elise supplied.

"Very. We've all tried to help, but we haven't had much success." Maggie beamed at her. "That's why we're so happy you're here."

"Oh, well." It was, Elise realized, past time for her to make something clear. "I haven't actually taken the job."

Maggie's smile dimmed. "But you *are* going to take it, aren't you?"

"That's undecided, I'm afraid. I don't usually accept jobs with single fathers. Things can get a bit sticky, and…" Now it was Elise's turn to trail off.

Why was she telling a woman she'd just met her personal business? She wasn't sure. There was something about this Maggie that made you feel you could tell her anything.

"Oh!" Relief flooded into Maggie's face. "I understand, but honestly, you wouldn't have anything to worry about with Ryder. For one thing, our mother, Ruby, would jerk a knot in him if he tried anything funny." Maggie's eyes twinkled. "And my two sisters and I would help her do it. But he's one of the good guys, promise."

"Who's one of the good guys? What are you two talking about?" Ryder asked suspiciously as he and the twins walked up to the table.

Elise felt a flush creeping up her cheekbones. Maggie, on the other hand, didn't seem the least bit embarrassed. She jumped up and gave her brother a hug. "I'm telling Elise what a great person you are, so she'll take this job."

"If you really want to help, find me an affordable place to rent that has separate living quarters for Elise. Have you heard of anything like that around here?"

"No. But wait a second." Maggie rapped her knuckles on the table. "Hey!" she called over the buzz of conversation in the bakery. "Anybody know of a place for rent that has a separate apartment with it? Like a mother-in-law suite or something?"

Most of the customers shook their heads, but one older woman in a pretty floral blouse spoke from a corner table.

"Abby Daniels is selling her house on Hickory Street. Just went on the market last week. Beverly Hall is the real estate agent."

"Oh." Maggie's eyes lit up. "Thanks, Lydia! That place would be perfect, Ryder. It's got the sweetest little cottage out in the backyard, all self-contained. Abby's mother lived there for years."

"I'll call Beverly now." Ryder pulled out his phone.

"It's for sale, not for rent, though," called the customer. "Now that her mama's passed, Abby's moving to Kentucky to be closer to her children."

"Don't you worry," Maggie assured Elise with a smile. "Ryder will figure out some way to make a deal. He always does." To Elise's astonishment, the other woman leaned over and gave her a warm, one-armed hug. "I'm so glad we've worked this out! We're going to be good friends, you and me. I just know it!"

Ryder got off the phone and turned to Elise. "I have the lockbox code. Hickory Street's a little too far to walk, but it's only about a five-minute drive. Want to go out and take a look, see if this place might solve our problem?"

"Sure she does!" Maggie answered for her. "I'll just pop those cookies in a bag, and you can take them with you!"

She bustled back toward the counter, leaving Elise feeling stunned. Ryder was right—Maggie was indeed a force to be reckoned with. She was like a friendly, redheaded hurricane—who smelled of vanilla and cookie dough.

"So?" Ryder prodded, and Elise blinked at him.

"I suppose we could go look," she agreed cautiously.

"Great!" He smiled, and that dimple twinkled at her again. "I'll drive."

Chapter Three

The house was adorable.

Elise got out of the car, her eyes fixed on the prim Victorian sitting in the middle of a large lawn. The yard—or garden, as Nanny Bev would call it—was a bit shaggy, but Elise liked it all the better for that. A few pleasant afternoons of tidying up, and it would be perfect.

A promising cottage peeked around the back of the house. It had its own little drive, and it was painted the same pretty cream color as the house itself. It even had a tiny porch, sheltering a wooden rocker with a fat blue cushion. She imagined herself sitting there early on a summer morning, enjoying her first cup of tea as she studied her daily devotional.

It made an appealing picture.

Another tick in the take-this-job column. Those were adding up.

She nodded at the For Sale sign on the lawn. "Is that negotiable?" she asked. "You're only looking for a rental, right?"

Ryder was opening the car door for the boys. "Everything's negotiable," he assured her with an easy smile.

A warning tickled in her stomach. That was exactly the sort of thing her father would have said. Andrew Cooper never doubted he'd get his way in the end.

"Here." Ryder checked his phone, then scribbled a series of numbers on a scrap of paper and handed them to her. "The cottage has its own lockbox. Put in this combination, and it'll open so you can get the key. While you look around out there, the boys and I will explore the house."

"All right." She waited until he'd herded the boys up the curved brick steps of the main house. Then she turned toward the cottage.

It looked like something from a storybook, with a dusty blue door and matching shutters around the generous windows. The porch was just big enough for the rocker and a terra-cotta pot holding a droopy geranium.

She stroked its fuzzy leaves as she went by. She'd give it a squirt of water before she left, she decided.

The lockbox yielded the key on her first try,

and the door opened easily. It was as if this little house was glad to see her.

Don't be silly, she told herself as she stepped inside.

She tried her best to look around critically, but there wasn't much to be critical about. It was small, but she preferred cozy houses. It had high ceilings that added to the sense of space, and ceiling fans in the three main rooms. They each whirred to life obediently when she flicked a switch.

There was a small sitting room, a kitchen with scaled-down appliances and a bedroom with an adjoining bath. It was furnished with some nice bits of old-fashioned furniture, and a faint smell of lemon cleanser lingered in the air.

The crisp scent reminded her of Nanny Bev, and she smiled sadly.

This snug place would have been perfect for Nanny Bev. She hadn't wanted to go into the assisted living facility, but after her last fall, it had seemed the wisest choice. Elise sighed.

"You don't like it?"

She turned to find Ryder standing in the doorway. The boys were nowhere in sight, but she could hear happy whoops in the background.

"Benji and Tucker discovered a big wooden swing set in the backyard," he explained. "It even has a fort, so they're having a blast. Tell me what's wrong with the house, and I'll find a way to fix it. If you accept this job—and I really hope you will—I want you to be completely happy."

In spite of her lingering concerns, her heart warmed. This man's determination to hire her was flattering—and a much-needed encouragement, after being left in the lurch by the Shermans. Their decision to accept the summer assignment in France offered by Jon Sherman's employer—who also happened to be a member of Andrew Cooper's college fraternity—had left her father smugly triumphant.

See? he'd gloated when he'd called to remind her of his invitation to spend the summer at Charleston. *You've worked for them for four years, but when it's in their best interests, they dump you like a bad habit. Your loyalty is misplaced, Elise. Always has been. You cared about your nanny more than your own father.*

"Elise?" Ryder was frowning at her. "If this doesn't suit you, we can scrap this idea and look for something else. Although I have to say, it might take an act of Congress to get those kids to give up that swing set."

"Sorry. No, the cottage is perfect. I was just thinking about my own former nanny. Nanny Bev's in an assisted living home in England now, but she would have loved a place like this."

"You had a nanny growing up?" He sounded surprised.

Elise winced. That wasn't information she normally shared with her employers. People sometimes reacted strangely when they realized she didn't have the working-class background they expected.

"Yes, I did. My mother died when I was a baby, and my father's job was very demanding."

"And she's from England?"

"That's right."

He laughed. "That solves the riddle. You have an odd British inflection here and there. I was wondering where it came from. It's nice," he added quickly. "And probably an asset in your profession, I'd think."

He was right, actually. "My clients do like it. I think it makes them feel a bit posh. That's a change. People used to make fun of the way I talked in school, but I never cared. I liked using British expressions because they reminded me of Nanny Bev."

"You miss her." It wasn't a question. He sounded as if he understood.

"I do. I wish I could have her close by and take care of her—the way she took care of me when I was growing up. If I could, I'd buy her a little house just like this one."

"I know what you mean." One side of his

mouth tipped up in a smile. "For me, it's my foster mom, Ruby. She took care of me when nobody else would. That little woman saved my life, and she didn't stop with me. She did that for all the rest of them, too." He shook his head. "Six times. She pulled kids out of the worst possible situations six times. Not many people have the courage—or the stubbornness—to do that, but she did. If that little woman told me a rock from the moon would look pretty on her fireplace mantel, I'd start building a spaceship. It's the people who love us when nobody else does—when we're the most unlovable…those are the people you never forget." His jaw firmed up. "I want to give that to the boys, if I can."

Oh, she was sunk. She knew it as soon as she saw that glint of hopeful determination shining in the man's eyes.

"I only have the summer," she heard herself saying. "When the Shermans get back from Europe at the end of August, they expect me to come back to work for them."

"Understood." He held out his hand. "So? Do we have ourselves a deal?"

She hesitated, although she already knew perfectly well what she was going to say. "We have a deal," she said, shaking his hand. "I mean, assuming you can work something out with the owner of this property."

"Already done. I called her as soon as I'd looked over the house. She's renting it to me furnished for the summer."

Elise raised an eyebrow. "I thought she only wanted to sell it."

"Like I said, everything's negotiable." He smiled. "And I can be pretty persuasive when I put my mind to it."

She didn't smile back. He'd only been in the house about ten minutes, so the phone call couldn't have lasted long. And yet he'd come out with a deal that suited him, but that didn't sound at all like what the landlady had wanted.

Her father used his charm to cut deals like that, too. Elise chewed on the inside of her lip. Maybe this hadn't been such a great idea after all.

"Come on," Ryder was saying. "Let's go see if I can use those skills of persuasion to detach the boys from the swing set. We need to get you back to your car. The sooner you go back home and pack up, the sooner you'll be back here and ready to start work. And Elise?" He caught her gaze and held it. "Thank you." He smiled, that single dimple twinkling in his cheek.

Elise pressed her lips together in a tight professional line and straightened her shoulders. "Of course," she said crisply, pointedly ignoring the warm, mushy feeling in her stomach. "I'll be ready to begin work as soon as I've reviewed and signed the contract."

"Oh! Right. I'll have to get one drawn up." Ryder's smile faded.

Just as well. He could save that dimple and all those charming powers of persuasion for somebody else—for two reasons. First, because he was starting to remind her unpleasantly of the "up-and-coming" young executives her father had pushed in her direction over the last few years.

And second, because, as it happened, Ryder Montgomery was quite mistaken.

Everything most certainly was *not* negotiable.

Three long days later, Ryder pulled into the driveway of his temporary home, put the car in Park and leaned his forehead against the steering wheel. The screaming in the back seat got louder, but at the moment he didn't care.

He kinda felt like screaming himself.

He'd had no idea buying clothes for the twins would be so stinking complicated. He'd just wanted to buy a few pairs of shorts and some shirts. Seriously, how hard could that be?

Turned out it could be more than hard. It could be impossible.

The kids had run amok in the department store. They'd grabbed things off racks, wouldn't try anything on, hidden from him and refused to come out when he called. They'd nearly given him a heart attack.

He'd finally located them when he'd heard a commotion from the ladies' department. He'd sprinted in that direction and discovered the boys ducking under the doors of the women's dressing rooms—many of which were occupied.

Ryder had apologized profusely, scooped up the twins and left the store without buying so much as a pair of socks.

He should have waited. Elise was due to arrive later today, and no doubt if she'd been along, the shopping trip would have gone a lot smoother.

Yeah, waiting would have made a lot more sense. But that little comment Maggie had made about the boys looking like ragamuffins had bugged him.

It had also been embarrassing, especially since she'd said it in front of Elise.

He'd already felt a little off-kilter. She was amazing with the boys, of course. But before he'd seen her photo, he'd expected a plump, gray-haired motherly person, and Elise was not only young—probably around his age—but really attractive. Plus, she had that air of crisp professionalism down pat. No doubt she was used to working for wealthy families whose kids never had torn collars or scuffed-up shoes.

As if that hadn't been intimidating enough,

then she'd mentioned she'd grown up with a nanny herself—a British nanny who'd covered for a dad with a demanding job. Elise had probably never had a torn collar either.

Well, he didn't want her—or anybody else—thinking he didn't care enough to make sure the twins had what they needed. He'd always been that kid back in school—the one whose clothes were ripped and dirty.

The one whose dad couldn't have cared less.

He was no superstar in the parenthood department, but he could at least see that Tuck and Benji had decent clothes, clothes that nobody could point at or make fun of. So he'd figured he'd take the kids shopping before Elise got back, and when she arrived, they'd be decked out in nice matching outfits.

Well, so much for that idea. He sighed, raised his head—and blinked. A silver compact car was tucked up next to the cottage in the side yard.

An overwhelming feeling of relief washed over him. Elise had arrived early. Now things would start looking up.

Finally.

"Nanny Elise is here!" he shouted over the chaos in the back seat.

The boys' screaming stopped abruptly. For a few precious seconds there was absolute silence in the car. Then, "Can we go see her?" Benji asked.

"I guess so."

A few seconds later, the boys were running across the grass to the cottage.

"Guys, hold up! We have to knock. She might be—" As usual, the twins paid no attention to him. The minute they reached the door, they pushed it open and barged right in.

It was the dressing rooms all over again. Ryder braced himself for an explosion…but nothing happened.

When he reached the doorway, Elise was standing in her little living room smiling down at the boys. After the disaster back in the department store, he was thankful to see that she was fully dressed in a pair of cream slacks and a pretty peach-colored top. Today her hair was pulled over to one side in a ponytail, trailing over her shoulder, and she held a book in one hand, marking her place with a finger.

"Well," she said with a laugh. "That was an enthusiastic welcome."

"Sorry," Ryder apologized. "I told them to knock, but—"

"Ah, yes." She nodded sagely. "Knocking is very important. Why don't we practice that? Go outside, boys, and close the door."

The boys looked at each other. "But we wanna see your house. Uncle Ryder wouldn't let us in here before. And the door was locked," Benji complained.

"The windows, too," Tucker added.

Ryder frowned. When had the boys done a recon on the cottage? He'd been watching them every second.

Or he thought he had.

"I'll be happy to give you the tour." When Benji attempted to slip past her into the kitchen, she gently restrained him by one shoulder. "As soon as you knock politely. Out you go." She sounded cheerful and firm, and to Ryder's astonishment, the boys backed outside, standing with him on the porch. "Shut the door, please." They did. "All right. Knock whenever you're ready."

Both boys raised fists and pounded on the door as if they were about to conduct some kind of police raid.

"Who is it?" Elise called in a sweet, slightly muffled voice.

"Tucker!"

"Benji!" The boys called out their names at the same time.

"Just a minute!" Elise opened the door and peered down at the boys with a smile. "What a delightful surprise. Please come in." The boys walked inside, looking pleased with themselves. "Would you like to see the cottage?" When they nodded, she said, "Then come this way!"

Ryder trailed behind while she gave them the tour. He'd only gotten a quick glimpse of this place before. It had seemed nice enough then, but it already had a different feel to it.

A different smell, too—a fresh scent that reminded him of clean laundry. The old bedspread had been replaced by a comforter in summery shades of turquoise and cream, and matching throw pillows were angled against the headboard. A bouquet of daisies in a fat blue vase graced the center of the tiny kitchen table, and several books were stacked beside the easy chair in the living room.

He scanned the titles and raised an eyebrow. He and Elise Cooper shared the same taste in authors.

"Would you like some lemonade?" She opened the small refrigerator and pulled out a plastic pitcher. "It's a hot day, and you all look a bit flushed. A nice cold drink and a light lunch would hit the spot, I think. Are you hungry?" When the boys nodded, she settled them at the little round kitchen table.

"What are them things?" Benji asked, pointing toward the counter where a small polished stand displayed two miniature flags.

Elise picked it up and set it on the table. "This is the United States flag, and this one is England's flag," she explained.

The boys were fascinated. "We seen that one before," Tuck said, pointing to the American flag. "But why you got two?"

She smiled. "Because both places are very special to me. I take these flags with me wherever I go, and they remind me of all the people I care about and all my happy memories here in the U.S. and in England."

The twins appeared satisfied with that explanation. A second later, they were happily munching on cheese cubes, pretzels and sliced grapes.

It wasn't macaroni and cheese, but nobody was flinging anything. Amazing.

She handed Ryder a glass of lemonade. "You look like you could use a cool drink, too."

"Thanks." Since there were no more seats in the kitchen, she motioned toward the living room. He sat on the love seat, and Elise positioned herself in the easy chair where she could keep an eye on the twins at the table.

He should have done that himself, he realized belatedly. That same feeling of guilty relief washed over him. It was wonderful to have help looking out for the boys for a change—somebody who had a clue what they were doing.

"I hope you don't mind that I let myself in," Elise was saying. "I waited a few minutes on the front porch, but since I wasn't sure when you'd get back, I thought I might as well get settled."

"That's fine. Sorry I wasn't here. I'd taken the boys shopping for some new clothes."

"Did you? Excellent." She nodded approvingly. "I was planning to see to that first thing, but now I can check it off the list."

He avoided her gaze, feeling ridiculously embarrassed. "Afraid not. It didn't go so well. We came home empty-handed." In a low voice, he recounted the events at the department store as Elise listened, her face carefully blank. He couldn't tell if she was shocked or not.

When he'd finished speaking, she cleared her throat. "I see. Did the boys want to go shopping today?"

It seemed like an odd question. "No. As a matter of fact, they wanted to stay here and play in the backyard."

She drew in a long, slow breath. "Well," she said. "Then as soon as they've finished their lunch, we'd best go back to the store and try again."

"What? Like, today?" He wasn't entirely sure the store would even allow them back in.

"Definitely." She spoke with a firm certainty. "Tucker and Benji have learned that if they cause enough trouble, grown-ups get frustrated and stop trying to make them behave. That's a lesson they have to unlearn quickly." She offered him a brief smile. "You don't have to go with us. I'll need some way to pay for the clothes, but—"

"I'll go." He didn't want to. But he also didn't want his nephews to think they could manipulate him by acting like little terrors. How had he missed that?

"No need to keep a dog and do your own barking," Elise was saying. "I'm perfectly capable of handling the boys on my own. There's…um… even a possibility they might behave better with only me in charge."

Ouch. But he knew she was right.

"You'll be in complete charge. I'll just watch. I think it's high time this mutt had a barking lesson."

She didn't look convinced, but she nodded. "If that's what you want."

"It is." He stood up. "Let's go."

The boys weren't happy about being dragged back to Dutch's Department Store. They began to kick up a fuss, but Elise headed them off at the pass. If they didn't have nice clothes, she told them, they wouldn't be able to go on the fun outings she had planned. Plus, they needed sturdy shoes to enjoy the backyard fort. Otherwise, they'd be stuck inside all summer. However, since the house probably needed top to bottom cleaning, they could certainly help her with that instead.

Two sulky boys were in the car in five minutes. Elise settled herself in the front seat, her hands clasped neatly in her lap.

"You sure made that look easy," Ryder muttered. This was embarrassing.

"Not easy," she corrected quietly. "Simple, maybe. Once you understand children, anyway. But it's never easy." She pulled a pad out of her purse and began jotting notes.

"What are you doing?"

"Making a list of what the boys need. I'm assuming pretty much everything. Am I right?"

He hated to admit it, but she was. "Yeah. They didn't bring much with them." And what they had brought hadn't been worth keeping.

Elise cleared her throat. "May I ask what budget we're working with? I don't want to overspend."

"Don't worry about that. Just get what they need."

"All right." She made a few more scribbles. "Part of shopping successfully with young children is speed. Having lists and budgets settled ahead of time helps. We'll make this as quick and painless as possible."

She meant what she said. He watched in awe as she rapidly went through the store, outfitting one twin after another. Underwear, socks, shorts, shoes and shirts. She offered no choice on most things, he noticed, but she did allow the boys to decide if they wanted shirts the same color or not, and if they wanted dinosaurs or spaceships on their pajamas.

She was brisk, firm and seemed to know instinctively where everything was located in the store. She also gave the boys jobs—each of them was given a plastic shopping basket to carry his own items. This, Ryder noticed, had the happy side benefit of keeping their hands safely occupied.

He tried to be helpful, but there wasn't much for him to do. In twenty minutes, the cashier was ringing up the purchases. He didn't know whether to feel grateful or humiliated. She'd certainly bested him in the shopping-with-kids category.

He had a feeling he'd better get used to that.

He reclaimed his debit card as Elise gathered up the bags and boxes. She distributed some of the smaller bags between the twins, and they started toward the door.

The twins, as usual, were leading the way, and as Tucker passed through the security scanner, an alarm blared. The little boy's face flushed red.

"I didn't take nothing!"

"Don't worry." Ryder reached for the bag. "They probably just left one of the security tags on. We'll figure it out." He rummaged through the sack, looking for the offending item.

"Tucker." Elise spoke quietly. "What do you have in your pocket?"

Ryder froze and looked up. She was holding his nephew's gaze, her eyebrows lifted. Tucker's face puckered as if he were going to cry.

"I ain't got nothing," he insisted, looking ashamed and miserable.

Unhappy memories from Ryder's own childhood stirred to life—and kicked him squarely in the gut.

He knew exactly how Tucker felt right now, and he put a comforting hand on the boy's shoulder. "This is a mistake."

"Yes, it's a mistake." Elise's voice was calm but firm. "Stealing always is. Tucker, empty your pocket, please." She held out her hand.

"Oh, good grief. He didn't take anything. He's four," Ryder said. "And we were with him every second."

Elise didn't answer. She wiggled her fingers. "Tucker."

The child dug reluctantly into his pocket, pulling out a gold bracelet. A plastic security tag dangled from its clasp.

Ryder's heart dropped to his shoes. There'd been a display of those on a table near the checkout counter. The kid must have swiped it when nobody was looking.

"Give it to me, please," Elise said. Slowly

Tucker placed it in her palm. Elise turned to look at the cashier. "Ma'am, would you be kind enough to get your store manager? It seems we need to make an apology."

Ryder barely heard her. He was still looking at Tucker. The child's face was bright red, and he was fighting tears. Ryder's heart twisted.

Oh, yeah, he knew that feeling, all right. Suddenly he was seven years old again, with a hungry stomach and a pocket full of stolen candy, being yelled at by a convenience store manager. He'd called the cops, *to make an impression*, the manager had said. Ryder had ended up riding to the station in the back of a patrol car.

Benji grabbed his twin's hand and looked up, his face horrified. "Uncle Ryder, don't let them put Tuck in jail. *Please*."

"Nobody's going to jail," Elise said. "We just need to—"

"Pay for that bracelet," he interrupted. "Give it to me."

"Ryder." Elise shot him a loaded look, reminding him wordlessly about his promise that she'd be the one in charge.

He hesitated, but another look at Tucker's tear-filled eyes made the decision for him.

He set his jaw, scooped the trinket from her palm and handed it to the cashier.

"Ring that up."

Chapter Four

He was in trouble.

Ryder shot a wary look in Elise's direction. She was sitting stiffly in the passenger seat of his car, her expression set firmly on neutral. She hadn't said a word since they'd left the store.

Even the twins were quiet—for once. Normally, Ryder would've counted that a blessing, but right now, it just made the chilly silence in the car seem even louder.

He didn't blame her for being mad. He'd stepped in and overruled her after assuring her she'd be in charge. He'd have been irritated, too.

But he'd had no choice. Maybe he didn't know beans about parenting, but he knew plenty about getting into trouble. He knew how it felt to have critical eyes on you. How easy it was to believe deep down that the angry grown-ups were right. You were a lost cause.

Tucker and Benji had driven him bonkers, and they sure weren't going to win any good citizenship awards anytime soon, but no kid should feel like that.

So, yeah. Maybe he'd made some big parenting blunder. But that look of grateful relief in Tucker's eyes when Ryder had pulled out his wallet and paid for the bracelet had been worth it.

At least, he hoped so.

He just wasn't sure how he was going to explain all that to Elise. Given her background, he seriously doubted she'd understand. One thing was for sure, though. Judging by that look on her face, he'd better find some way to mend his fences—and fast. He massaged his forehead wearily as they waited their turn at a stop sign.

The drive to the house took only about ten minutes, but it seemed longer. Ryder breathed a sigh of relief as the car rolled up the drive.

Elise busied herself with unbuckling her seat belt, carefully avoiding his eyes. "I'll take the boys' new clothes inside and put them in the wash. That should take a few minutes, and it'll give you some privacy for your talk with Tucker." She shot him a brief look. "I'm assuming you'll want to have a chat about what happened at the store."

She pronounced *privacy* like the Brits, with a

short *i* sound. Ryder registered that fact in the back of his worried brain.

It was cute.

What wasn't so cute was the prospect of the discussion he was supposed to have with his nephew. He'd figured this thing was settled—for better or worse.

Apparently not.

"Guys, go play in the backyard, okay? I'll be right behind you. Elise, could we talk?"

"If you like." She was gathering up the bags from the trunk. "Although personally I wouldn't allow the boys to play until this matter has been dealt with. Mind you," she added dryly, "that's just my opinion."

Which you don't seem to have much respect for. She didn't say that part aloud, but she might as well have.

"Here, let me carry those for you." He reached for the bags, but she stepped backward and shook her head.

"I'm perfectly capable of carrying them myself." For the first time since they'd left the department store, she looked him in the eye. "I'm here to do a job, remember. Things might go more smoothly if you allow me to do it."

He winced. "Okay, I deserved that. And, of course, I want you to do your job. What happened at the store was a…knee-jerk reaction." He wasn't sure how to explain this. For some reason, he felt reluctant to share all the sordid details of his childhood with this clear-eyed woman.

"Those aren't always wise."

"Maybe not." For the first time, annoyance sparked. "But they're not always dead wrong, either."

"I see." She studied him. "I really should get these clothes in the wash. We'll finish this discussion later and decide how we want to proceed."

Well, that sounded ominous.

As he walked ahead of her to unlock the door, Ryder felt a rising tide of panic. "Elise? To be honest, I'm not sure exactly what I'm supposed to say to Tuck. Do you have any tips?"

She paused, looking at him frostily. "I'm sorry, but no, I'm afraid I don't. When you disregard my advice and get yourself into a pickle, it's not my responsibility to get you out of it."

With that parting shot, she disappeared into the house.

He sighed as he closed the door behind her. Yeah. He was definitely in trouble. The sooner he got back into Elise's good graces, the better. The boys needed her help—and so did he.

Ryder walked around the house, thinking hard. He paused under the shade of a blooming crepe myrtle and made a phone call.

A couple of expensive minutes later, he shoved the phone back into his pocket. There. He'd done his best. In fact, he'd ramped up his go-to apology strategy considerably—hopefully that would do the trick. Time to tackle his next problem.

The talk.

Pushing open the small gate, he walked into the backyard. For once the boys weren't chasing each other around with sticks, yelling at the top of their lungs, or throwing rocks at imaginary dinosaurs. They were swinging like perfectly behaved kids. When they saw him, they dragged their sneakers in the dusty grooves in the grass, slowing to a stop.

Ryder dropped onto the back step, stretching his legs out into the grass. For a second, he toyed with the idea of sending an SOS call to his brother Logan. Surely a sheriff could get this point across better than he could.

However, he suspected the first point Logan would get across was that this was Ryder's job to handle.

"Tuck, come over here, please. We need to talk."

Tucker and Benji exchanged glances. Tucker jumped out of the swing and trudged toward him, Benji following a few paces behind. Both twins looked worried, which was another change— and a good one. Up until now, they'd shrugged off their misbehavior, never caring how irritated people got with them.

That wasn't the only difference he saw. Tuck had actually come the first time he'd called him. Elise had barely been here any time, and the twins' behavior had already improved. He wasn't sure exactly why—but the stark contrast between their two shopping expeditions had made things pretty clear.

When it came to managing kids, this woman had some serious skills. He hoped his attempt to make amends worked. If it didn't, he'd figure out something that would. Whatever it took—that was his motto in sales, and he was prepared to pull out all the stops to keep Elise on board, too.

But first he had something else to worry about. Ryder studied Tucker's face and tried to think of the best way to approach this.

I could use some help here, God. I don't know what's the right thing to say. Ruby had taught him that prayers didn't need to be long or fancy. Hers certainly never were, and over the years he'd had a front row seat to seeing a lot of them answered in some pretty amazing ways.

"Tuck," he started. Then he stopped short. He'd been about to do a little preaching on the evils of stealing, but from the resigned looks on the boys' faces, they were expecting that.

They'd probably heard it all before anyway.

He'd sure heard more than his share of you'd-better-straighten-up-and-fly-right lectures before coming to Ruby's—so many that he'd perfected the art of tuning them out. He'd seen little reason to listen. None of the people doing the talking had cared about him. He'd known because they'd never bothered to find out anything about his life or why—

An idea occurred to him.

"Tuck? Why'd you take that bracelet?"

Nobody had ever asked Ryder why—not once. Not until Ruby. From the confused look on Tucker's face, nobody'd asked him before now, either.

"I dunno." The little boy shuffled his feet in the grass. "'Cause I wanted it, I guess."

"Why didn't you ask for it, then? We were buying lots of things in the store. We could have bought that, too."

"I couldn't ask *out loud*." Tucker shot him an exasperated glance.

"Why not?"

"It was 'posed to be a surprise."

In spite of himself, Ryder snorted a laugh. "It was a surprise, all right. When that alarm went off, I nearly jumped out of my skin."

Benji, who was watching this conversation from a safe distance, looked relieved that Ryder was laughing, but Tucker's frown deepened.

"I didn't want to surprise *you*." He kicked a tuft of grass. "I wanted to surprise her."

Ryder's eyebrows drew together as he studied his nephew. "Nanny Elise? You wanted the bracelet for her?"

"I thought maybe she'd like it." Tucker dropped his eyes, flushing miserably. "Mama woulda liked it. It was shiny."

"Mama liked shiny stuff," Benji volunteered sadly.

Ryder's heart constricted. Maybe his sister had struggled with her own problems, but her little sons had obviously loved her.

That told him a lot.

It also might explain the boys' sudden shift in behavior where Nanny Elise was concerned. He chewed on the inside of his cheek, at a loss for what to say next.

He should scold Tucker, probably. Expound on the evils of theft, no matter why you wanted the shiny bracelet. Shake his finger warningly, and end with *this better not happen again.*

But he found he couldn't do it. The truth was, this had dredged up a memory he'd half forgotten.

He'd been fifteen, and he'd walked past an appliance store with a brand-new washing machine in the window. That morning, Ruby's ancient washer had sprung a leak, made a loud grinding noise and died, in the middle of a busy laundry day. They'd mopped up sudsy water with bath towels, and Ruby had fished out the laundry to rinse in the sink. She hadn't fussed too much about it, but for the first time, Ryder had thought his beloved foster mom looked...old.

The minute he'd seen that gleaming new machine, a fierce desire had risen up in him. He'd wanted that washing machine for Ruby more than he'd ever wanted anything in his life.

If he could have stuffed it in his pocket and walked away with it, he'd have done it in a minute.

Frustrated, he rubbed at his forehead. This parenting stuff was tough.

"Is Nanny Elise real mad at me?"

He glanced up to find Tucker studying him. The little boy's mouth was trembling, and Ryder's heart dipped.

"She's upset, but mostly with me because I didn't...uh...listen too well. Come here." Ryder patted the bricks of the step. "You too, Benji."

Ryder thought Tucker would refuse, but after a brief hesitation, the boy walked over and dropped down on the step beside his uncle. Benji followed suit.

Ryder draped his arms over the boys' shoulders. The twins held themselves stiff and didn't lean against him, but they didn't jerk away, either.

He counted that a win.

"Here's the deal, guys. Stealing's wrong, and we don't do it. Period. From now on, if you want something, you can't just take it. You ask me. That goes for you, too, Benji."

Both boys looked at him with interest. Benji spoke first. "If we ask you, you gonna buy it for us?"

Oops.

"I can't promise that. It depends on what it is and how much it costs."

"Mama told us you had lotsa money," Benji murmured. It sounded like an accusation. "She said you wasn't poor like her."

Ryder's heart constricted. He should've done more to find Carrie after she'd dropped out of that last rehab—and off the radar. He'd just been so frustrated. He'd pulled a lot of strings and forked over a substantial sum of his very hard-earned money to get her into that place, and she'd walked out after a week and a half. He'd told himself he was done.

But if he'd tried to find her, maybe he'd have known about the twins. They must have been born only a year or so after he and Carrie had lost touch. If he'd known, he could have helped out before things got too bad.

Things might have turned out different.

He cleared his throat.

"I have some money, but not lots. Correction," he said quickly. "*We* have some, but not lots. What I have is yours now, too, but we have to be responsible with it."

He had the twins' full attention. They both sat up straighter.

"'Cause we got to pay bills," Benji volunteered. "Good stuff costs money. Like a house and a swing set with a fort. If you don't pay, then you got to leave in a hurry when it's dark outside."

"We done that lotsa times," Tucker added. "When Mama didn't have no money."

Ryder had to swallow twice before he could answer. "That's not going to happen anymore. We're always going to pay, so we won't have to leave until we're good and ready. Don't worry about that. But no more stealing."

"Because it makes Nanny Elise real mad," Benji supplied helpfully.

"It upsets her," Ryder corrected him. "Because it's wrong."

"I won't do it no more," Tucker said. "Promise. Can we go play now?"

Ryder blinked.

Was that it? Was this talk over with? He guessed so. He couldn't think of anything else to say.

All in all, that had gone a lot smoother than he'd expected.

"Sure, go ahead. It's getting kind of hot out here. I'll go inside and grab you guys some water bottles, okay?"

"Okay," the boys chorused as they ran off toward the swing set. Their usual energy was back, and they seemed cheerful again. He guessed life was pretty simple when you were four years old.

All right. One problem down, one to go. He glanced at his watch. Another fifteen minutes, more or less, before his attempt at an apology should arrive. In the meantime he'd keep his distance and pray Elise wasn't the sort of woman who held grudges.

He got up to go inside and grab the twins' water—and found himself nose to nose with Elise, who was looking through the large window in the back door.

His heart sank. So much for keeping his distance. Looked like it was already time for talk number two.

Elise stepped away from the door, and Ryder came into the kitchen, looking every bit as uncomfortable as she felt herself. She doubted he felt as guilty, though.

She hadn't meant to eavesdrop on his talk with the twins. She'd unearthed the bracelet in the bottom of one of the bags of clothing, and she'd brought it down to hand it over.

If she were being honest, she had to admit she planned to do so with a disapproving look—sort of a two-for-one special.

She'd had her hand on the doorknob when she'd overheard Tucker asking if she was "really mad." Concern and curiosity had trumped good manners, and she'd lingered there, listening.

What she'd heard had made a great deal of her irritation with Ryder drain away. She'd guessed, of course, that the twins' lives must have been difficult before they'd come into their uncle's care, but hearing that confirmed in Tucker's own words had made her heart ache.

She didn't agree with how Ryder had handled the incident at the store, but she certainly understood better now why he'd stepped in.

"Hi," he offered quickly. "I was just going to grab a couple of water bottles for the boys."

"Good idea. It's a hot day." She cleared her throat. "The boys' clothes are in the washer. Once they're dry, I'll put them away." She tilted the tiny bag over the oak table, and the bracelet tumbled out. "I wasn't quite sure what to do with this."

She'd skipped the disapproving look, but Ryder winced anyway.

"I have no idea. Look," he went on in a rush. "I talked with Tucker about what happened. I don't know if I did it right or not, but—"

"I think you did quite well. I…um…heard the last bit." She cleared her throat. "It sounds as if the twins have had a lot of chaos in their lives. Plus, the loss of their mother is very fresh, and grief always impacts behavior. We *had* agreed that I was to take charge, but I can certainly understand now why you…" She hesitated. *Caved* was probably not the kindest word choice. "Felt that a gentle approach was more appropriate," she finished tactfully.

His face relaxed into relief. "I'm glad you understand. And don't feel bad. If this had happened with one of the kids you usually work with, your way of handling it would have made perfect sense."

She frowned. "What do you mean?"

He seemed surprised that she needed an explanation. "Well, if a rich kid shoplifts something, it's for thrills. That's different than what Tuck did."

A rich kid. Elise took a second to compose her answer. "I don't believe it's so different at all. Having a wealthy family doesn't erase a child's emotional problems. In fact, it sometimes causes them."

"Right." He looked at her with a puzzled expression. "I thought that's what I was saying. They're spoiled."

Spoiled. Oh, dear. "Actually, there are many

reasons why a child might feel the need to steal something. And yes, sometimes it stems from overindulgence. But I can assure you, wealthy parents inflict chaos on their children, too. Believe it or not, they also sometimes pass away and leave their sons and daughters grieving."

At her words, his expression shifted into a remorseful horror. "Like your mom. I'm so sorry, Elise. I put my foot in it, didn't I? Please forgive me. That was really thoughtless."

Elise's heart thumped. She'd been getting irritated, but there was something so…genuine in Ryder's expression. As if he was truly sorry he'd forgotten about her personal history.

It was…endearing.

"I wasn't talking about myself. Like I told you before, my mother died when I was a baby. I don't remember her."

The concern in his eyes didn't ebb. "My mom died before I could remember her, too. Somehow, I still missed her. And I imagine it's even harder for a girl not to have her mother. I'm sorry."

"Well. Thank you." For some reason, his kindness made ridiculous tears prickle at the back of her eyes. "You're very compassionate. Which is good, because the boys need a lot of that just now." She straightened her shoulders. "Of course, they also need limits and structure, and they have some very bad habits they'll have to unlearn.

And going forward, it's very important that you and I be on the same page when it comes to consequences. After all, you hired me because you were having difficulty managing the boys' behaviors. I can't help with that if you ignore my suggestions."

Ryder hesitated. "I see your point. I do. And I know you're the expert, but there are a few things about my nephews I may understand better than you do." He smiled, and that dimple winked at her. "I think we'll make a good team, you and I. You've got the kid-whispering skills, and I understand what it's like to have a tough childhood."

She frowned. Team? She wasn't sure exactly what he meant by that. And no matter what he thought, her own childhood hadn't exactly been a walk in the park.

Before she could think of how best to explain that to him, the doorbell chimed.

Ryder glanced at his watch and smiled. "Right on time."

"What?"

"Nothing. Would you mind getting the door? I promised the boys I'd bring them out the water."

"I can do that." She started toward the fridge, but he stepped in front of her.

"No, I'll do it. You go get the door, and I'll be right back."

Before she could say anything else, he'd

grabbed two bottles from the refrigerator and headed outside. As she watched him striding across the yard, the doorbell chimed again, followed by an impatient series of bangs.

Elise frowned. Was this visitor—whoever it was—*kicking* the door of this beautiful house? That seemed rather rude.

Somebody needed a talking to.

She walked briskly through the house and pulled the front door open.

"Good aftern—" she started coldly, then stopped short.

She was talking to a wobbling wall of flowers. The entire doorway was crowded with blooms: roses, mums and lilies, interspersed with glossy ferns and white clouds of baby's breath.

"Ma'am?" A young woman's face appeared between a fern frond and a pink rose. "Are you Elise Cooper?"

"I...am."

"Good!" The relief in the woman's voice was palpable. "Then these are for you. And, um, they're kind of heavy, so if you wouldn't mind... moving aside a little so I could come inside and set them down?"

"I'm sorry." Hastily, Elise stepped back so the delivery person could pass. She had just enough presence of mind to scoot a stack of books sideways on the hall table, clearing a space for the mammoth arrangement.

The young woman thumped the flowers down in the empty spot and sighed. "Whew!" The young, freckled redhead turned to smile at Elise, wiping her hands on a bright green apron with the words Brenda's Blooms written in white script.

"Hi!" She stuck out one freshly cleaned hand. "I'm Brenda. Great to meet you, Elise."

"It's nice to meet you, too," Elise responded automatically, still staring at the huge bouquet.

Actually, huge was an understatement. She'd seen flowers at the front of cathedrals that weren't this impressive.

"Okay, don't keep me in suspense." Brenda tweaked a stray bloom into place. "I handled this order personally. What do you think?"

"They're…beautiful. They're…um…" Elise trailed off, shaking her head. "Wow."

"I know, right?" The woman chuckled. "Ryder insists on the wow factor. Not so easy to pull off this time, considering how quick he wanted me to get them here. I've never put an arrangement of this size together so fast. He must be in big trouble this time!"

"*Ryder* sent these? To me?"

The other woman winked. "Let the cat out of the bag there, did I? Although it wouldn't have been a mystery for long. There's a note tucked in there someplace. Don't forget to add some water to keep 'em fresh. I don't like to have too much in them when I'm transporting. Now I'd better get back to work. I had to set aside half a dozen flower arrangements headed to the maternity ward to get this one finished. Here." She fished in the pocket of her apron and pulled out a business card. "If you need any flowers while you're here, just give me a call."

Elise accepted the card. "Thank you, but I seem to be…rather well supplied for the moment."

The other woman laughed. "True." She bumped her shoulder chummily against Elise's. "I hope these'll help you forgive him for whatever he did. I'd sure like to be his go-to florist for his next apology—although you can warn him, he won't get near as good a discount on future orders. That boyfriend of yours sure knows how to sweet talk a deal."

"He's not my boyfriend," Elise protested quickly. "I'm only the nanny."

"Oh! Sorry, it's just that an arrangement like this… I assumed…" Brenda stumbled to a stop and shrugged. "Well, all I can say is, you must be some nanny! Have a great day, now!" With a cheerful wave, the woman bustled out the door, pulling it shut behind herself.

The house went silent, except for the sound of the florist's van starting up and the muffled shouts of the twins from the backyard. Elise scrutinized the oversize arrangement the way she'd study a strange dog before approaching, looking it over from every angle.

Her father had sent flower arrangements, too, usually after steamrolling over somebody's boundaries. He'd always believed that money and lavish gifts erased problems.

A tiny notecard peeped out of the foliage. She plucked it out and opened it. The message was short and straight to the point.

Sorry. I'll do better next time. Ryder.

Elise glanced from the card to the extravagant arrangement and back again as the florist's joking words echoed in her memory.

That boyfriend of yours.

Well, of course she'd think that. And soon she wouldn't be the only one. She'd heard that in small towns, gossip spread like wildfire.

Elise's mouth firmed up. It seemed the twins weren't the only ones who had some lessons to learn about proper behavior.

Chapter Five

❧

Leaving the enormous vase of blooms on the entry table, Elise walked back through the house. The shouts grew louder as she neared the backyard, and as soon as she went out onto the steps, she saw why. The twins were perched up in the fort, cheerfully pelting their uncle with various bits of debris and yelling at the top of their lungs.

"Okay, guys!" Ryder sounded exasperated. "Remember the rules. Throw leaves if you want to, but no sticks. No more rocks, either, Benji. I mean it!"

Even as his uncle spoke, Benji yanked a stick off the overhanging tree and lobbed it in Ryder's direction.

"That's it!" Ryder ducked as the stick whizzed by his head. "Game's over."

The boys ignored him, already scrabbling for something else to throw.

Elise scanned their flushed faces with a frown. At this point they were far too overexcited for their uncle's instructions to register. She set her jaw and headed across the yard. Once under the fort, she clapped her hands briskly.

"Benji, Tucker, come down immediately."

Two perspiring faces peered down at her from over the railing. "No! We're playing Uncle Ryder's King of the Castle game," Benji protested. "And we're winning. We ain't gonna—"

Before he could finish his sentence, Tucker gave him a push and muttered something. Benji's lips pooched out in a mulish pout, but he dropped the dirt clod he was holding and followed his twin to the ladder.

"How do you *do* that?" Ryder raked one hand through his hair, dislodging an acorn and three leaves.

She ignored the question. "This game was your idea?"

"Yeah." He looked embarrassed. "Sort of. In my defense, projectiles were never in the plan. Well. No big ones. And definitely no rocks."

Oh, for pity's sake. She shot him an exasperated look. "You and I will speak in a moment."

Both boys came to stand in front of her, grimy faces upturned. How on earth did children get so dirty so fast?

"You weren't listening to your uncle," she

pointed out firmly. "And you were throwing things you shouldn't have been. So this game is over."

"That ain't fair," Benji started hotly, but Tuck nudged his twin with one shoulder.

"You gotta do what she says," he whispered.

Benji shot his brother an irritated look.

"It's time for a snack," Elise announced. "Go inside and wash your hands and faces. With soap," she added firmly. "Then sit at the kitchen table. I'll be right in after I have a word with your uncle."

"What kinda snack?" Benji asked suspiciously.

"Oh, that don't matter," Tucker said quickly. "We can eat it."

Benji made a disgusted noise and trudged off toward the kitchen.

"Thank you, Tucker," Elise said. "I appreciate your good attitude."

"That's okay." The little boy flushed. "I'm sorry about what I done earlier. I won't steal no more. I promise."

"Anymore," she corrected gently. "And I'm very glad to hear it."

"You ain't going to leave. Are you?"

He looked up at her, his expression worried. Elise's heart twinged.

"Not until the end of the summer. Now go inside and wash up."

The end of summer was ages away to a four-year-old. Tucker grinned and ran toward the house. Elise watched him go, her lips pressed tightly together.

Oh, dear.

"Well," Ryder said as the door slammed behind the little boy. "That's a first. I don't think either of the twins have ever apologized before."

She turned to face him. "Maybe not, but he did it quite well. Simple and sincere." She paused and quirked an eyebrow. "Perhaps you should consider following his example."

"Excuse me?"

"Your flowers arrived."

"Oh, yeah!" Ryder's face brightened. "Do you like them?"

"Whether I like them or not is entirely beside the point. I can't accept them."

"You can't—why not?"

"Because they're inappropriate. I'm your employee, not your—" Surely she didn't need to spell this out. "Ours is a completely professional arrangement—in spite of what your florist seems to think."

An embarrassed horror dawned on Ryder's face. "Elise, I'm so sorry. I was in a hurry when I placed the order, and… I guess Brenda got the wrong idea."

"Understandable. That's a very extravagant gift to send an employee."

"Extravagant? Flowers?"

"Not just flowers. Half a truckload of flowers. I can only imagine what they cost."

"Not that much, honestly. Brenda cut me a deal."

"So she said. Among other things. But the fact is, I can't accept any gifts from you. Expensive or otherwise."

There was a short silence. "I understand."

Good. She straightened her shoulders. "I hope so. If our arrangement is going to work—"

"It has to work," he interrupted.

"Both of us have to follow professional guidelines," Elise finished doggedly.

He nodded. "I will. Got it. No more gifts, and I'll set Brenda straight the first chance I get." He shook his head. "Looks like Tucker and I both had a lesson to learn about gift-giving today. Sorry. My sisters love flowers, and I've fallen into the habit of sending them a *wow*-level arrangement whenever I get myself into trouble." He offered a smile. "Which, as you probably can imagine, is fairly often."

So that's who he sent flowers to. His sisters. Okay. That was rather sweet.

And absolutely none of her business.

"I'm sure they appreciate it. But I'm not your sister."

"No. You sure aren't."

She shot him a wary look. Strange how he said that so...definitively.

She decided to let it go. Something else he'd said was niggling at her. "What did you mean just then? About you and Tucker both learning a lesson about gift-giving?"

"The bracelet." He seemed to expect her to understand. When she just looked at him, he frowned. "Sorry, I thought you said you'd overheard our talk. He stole it for you."

"For me?" Elise's voice cracked. "No. I didn't hear that bit. Oh, dear."

This was even more concerning than she'd thought.

"Well, that's not so terrible, is it? Obviously, he went about it all wrong, but at least his heart was in the right place. He wanted to please you. That's a good thing, isn't it?"

Elise tried to think of how best to phrase her reply. "It can be."

"That's what I thought. I try to give Ruby gifts all the time. *Try* being the operative word. Of course, I buy them," he added with a chuckle. "I don't steal them. Not that it makes much difference."

Elise was intrigued in spite of herself. "She

doesn't like gifts?" Nanny Bev did—a tin of her favorite Darjeeling tea or a packet of lemon biscuits always brought a smile.

"She likes gifts okay. She just hates for us to spend our money on her." He shook his head. "I carved her a wooden spoon in high school, and she used the thing until it snapped apart in her hand. She still won't throw away the pieces. But when I tried to give her a dishwasher a couple years ago, she staged a standoff with the truck driver in her front yard. She wouldn't even let him unload it and demanded the company give me a full refund. They did, too. Ruby's a stubborn old bird."

A stubborn bird he was very fond of. She could hear it every time he spoke of her. "She sounds lovely."

In fact, she sounded a lot like Nanny Bev. Tea and biscuits were one thing, but if Nanny B. had any idea that Elise was helping pay for her assisted living expenses…well, she'd never stand for it. Elise and Nanny's faithful attorney had arranged for an anonymous "stipend" to cover the amount beyond Nanny's budget.

So far, she'd not been suspicious.

"Yeah," Ryder agreed with a smile. "She's stubborn *and* lovely." He cleared his throat. "Anyway, I think it's a good sign that Tuck wanted to give you something. It means he's getting attached to you, right?"

"Yes. But…" She hated to give him bad news, but she didn't have a choice. "That's likely to cause a different problem. We don't want him to get too attached to me. I'm only here for the summer. When I leave—"

Ryder's face fell. "When you leave, it'll be like losing his mom all over again. I should have thought of that."

"Well, don't worry. Now that I see the problem, I can work on solving it. It won't be the first time I've had to help a child sort out the difference between our relationship and the one he has with his parents. I'm actually quite good at that."

Ryder's frown reversed direction with flattering speed. "I can certainly believe that. You're downright amazing."

"I do my best."

The answer sounded prim and stiff, but it was all she could manage. There was something about the way Ryder was looking at her—his face alight with admiration and relief—that made a distracting, fluttery warmth expand in her chest.

She *did* do her best, always. She took her vocation seriously, and she had Nanny Bev's excellent example to follow as well as the benefit of some high-quality training. The parents who employed her were usually quite satisfied with her performance—and she always received glowing letters of recommendation.

Still, she'd never felt so…*appreciated* as she did right now.

The uncertainty she'd felt since the florist delivery ebbed away. The flowers were a simple misunderstanding. Likely, this job would turn out all right after all. Once she, Ryder and the twins had established a solid routine, they'd all jog along just fine.

Speaking of that, it was high time to get that routine ironed out.

"I'd best get inside and serve up some snacks. After that, the boys and I will have some quiet time. I brought some books, and I thought we'd read aloud for a half hour this afternoon. It'll be calming after all of this morning's…excitement."

Ryder had the grace to look embarrassed—and impressed. "You're going to get the boys to sit still and listen to a story? That'll be a first. Story time at the library was a complete flop."

She nodded. "The book-throwing. I remember. The boys and I will be making a trip to the library in a day or so to mend fences. In the meantime, a lesson in how to enjoy quiet activities seems appropriate. Afterwards, we'll do a tidy up of their room. Then a nice walk, I think. That should keep us occupied until suppertime."

She started toward the house, and Ryder fell into step beside her.

"I'll cook," he volunteered. "I'm not exactly a chef, but I'll figure something out."

They hadn't worked out meals yet, but this seemed a sensible arrangement. "All right. I'll take charge of the boys' lunches and breakfasts. I expect that'll suit your schedule better, anyway."

"My schedule?"

"Your work schedule." She opened the door and glanced into the kitchen. Tucker was seated at the table, but Benji had his head in the refrigerator—and his hand on a jar of olives. Apparently she'd arrived not a moment too soon. "Benji, olives are not on our menu right now. Please put them back and sit down at the table." She glanced at Ryder. "I'll take charge of the boys for the rest of the afternoon. Going forward, I will supervise them from 7:00 a.m. to 7:00 p.m. each day except for Sunday. I assume that's acceptable, as per our contract?"

"Yeah, sure." He was frowning again.

"Very well." She smiled. "Now, I'm sure you have some important matters requiring your attention."

"Well, yeah." He nodded at the boys. "This."

"Excuse me?" Benji was still stubbornly fighting with the lid of the olive jar. She took it away and set it back in the refrigerator, then ushered the child firmly to his seat. She chose an apple from a bowl on the counter and went to the sink.

"*This* is what I'm planning to give my attention to this summer. You and the twins. I'll work at night when they're asleep, but during the day I'm planning to stick with you."

She turned to stare at him. "*Stick* with me?" What on earth could he mean?

"Sure. How else am I going to learn how to—" He gestured vaguely. "You know. Do what you do. I've got a lot to learn, so I'll be shadowing you from breakfast to bedtime." He smiled, and that all-too-beguiling lone dimple twinkled in his cheek. "Every day but Sunday."

"Oh." The apple slipped from Elise's suddenly clumsy fingers and thumped into the bottom of the sink. "Oh, *dear.*"

Later that evening, Ryder tapped his phone, bringing up the app connected to the monitor he'd installed in the boys' bedroom. The video on the small screen reassured him. Tucker and Benji were sprawled out on their twin beds, sound asleep. Good.

Getting the boys to bed was always a free-for-all, but once they zonked out, they stayed zonked until morning. That cleared him for the talk he needed to have with Elise.

She'd been frosty and stiff all evening, and

she'd barely touched her supper—even though the hamburgers he'd cooked on the gas grill outside had turned out not so bad. When the clock in the hall had chimed seven, she'd looked relieved—and left as quickly as she could.

He wasn't sure what was wrong. Maybe she wasn't over their shoplifting, flower-sending disaster of a day, or maybe it was something else.

He didn't know, but he intended to find out.

He walked across the moonlit yard toward her little cottage. The lights were shining warmly in the windows, giving off a welcoming glow. However, he suspected that—in this case, at least—looks were deceiving.

He doubted Elise was going to be glad to see him.

He knocked on the door and waited. He heard rustlings, and a few seconds later, she opened it a crack and peeked out at him.

Sure enough, she didn't look particularly overjoyed to see him on her doorstep.

"Is something wrong?" she asked.

"That would be my guess," he said. "I'm just not sure what it is. I thought maybe we should talk."

The concern on her face faded into weary apprehension. "I suppose we'd better." She opened the door. "Come in."

She'd changed into an oversized T-shirt in a

pretty shade of weathered red, and some black stretchy-looking pants. Her feet were bare, and her hair tumbled loose around her shoulders.

He had a hard time pulling his eyes away from her. In her work clothes, she'd projected a competent professionalism that—in all honesty—was a little bit intimidating. Now she radiated the kind of girl-next-door charm that he'd always found...well.

Irresistible.

He cleared his throat. "Sorry to bother you," he said. "I hope I'm not interrupting anything."

"I was reading." Sure enough, a mystery novel rested on the arm of the overstuffed chair, a bookmark carefully holding her place. A cup of tea waited on a handy table, still steaming, its gentle aroma scenting the air. A light, cream-colored throw was puddled on the floor.

She'd had a stressful day—thanks in large part to him—but she'd created peace and order in this room. He could see Elise cuddled up in the chair, her lips pursed in that pout of concentration he'd already learned to recognize, her eyes scanning the pages, absently sipping her tea.

The cozy image uncurled a hungry loneliness deep in Ryder's stomach. It would be...nice...he thought, to spend evenings in a room like this. Growing up, he'd been left alone at home a lot while his dad was out gambling. But at Ruby's, with six noisy kids crowded into a small home, he'd never been alone for very long.

That had been annoying sometimes, but nice, too.

He'd been living a pretty solitary life since moving to Atlanta, but that had changed when the twins arrived. Now, once again, alone time was hard to come by, but in another way, he was more alone than ever. He was solely responsible for the boys—a job that terrified him, and one that so far he wasn't particularly good at. His whole life had turned upside down. And his worries were multiplying like rabbits.

He'd never felt more alone in his life.

He wouldn't mind sitting here with Elise for an hour or two, watching her read, listening to the whisper of turning pages and the ticks of the clock on the wall, and soaking in this quiet contentment.

If they were friends, yeah. That would have been nice.

"I'm sorry. Did you want some tea?"

He blinked and came back to himself. Elise was studying him, her brows drawn together, probably wondering why he was staring at her teacup.

"No, thanks. May I sit?"

"Certainly."

Elise gestured toward the little love seat and

retreated to the armchair. As she sat, she tossed the lightweight blanket over her legs so her bare toes were hidden. Something about the prim sweetness of that gesture made Ryder smother a smile.

He took a seat, angling his phone on the cushion beside him so he could see the live feed of the boys as they talked. They probably wouldn't wake up, but if the last few weeks had taught him anything, it was to expect the unexpected where the boys were concerned.

And to keep a sharp eye on them.

She leaned forward, her hands clasped over her knees. "I'm glad you decided to come over," she said. "Because you're right. We do need to talk."

"I gathered that. You were pretty quiet all afternoon and during dinner." Pretty quiet was an understatement. She'd gone radio silent, and his concern had grown with every passing moment.

"I suppose I was. I'm sorry about that. I didn't know exactly how to explain things to you."

That didn't sound good. "Look, I'm really sorry about the flowers." She'd left the arrangement on the entryway table. She hadn't even taken the note. He'd thought she'd accepted his apology for that particular goof-up, but maybe not.

But she shook her head. "This isn't about the

flowers. It's about what you said later…about wanting to learn from me."

"Okay." Ryder blinked. He thought he'd been prepared for just about anything, but he hadn't seen that particular curveball coming. "What about it?"

"Well, it's a bit of a problem." She spoke calmly, but Ryder's people-reading skills were on high alert. She was clenching her fingers so tightly that her knuckles were pale. She was uneasy. "It's an admirable sentiment, of course."

An admirable sentiment. Once again, Ryder found himself fighting back an inconvenient smile. He didn't want her to think he was amused that she was uncomfortable—he wasn't. But sometimes this woman spoke like a Victorian greeting card. "Then what's the problem?"

"It's not what I do."

"Excuse me?"

She fiddled with the blanket as pink drifted into her cheeks. "I'm a nanny. I take care of children. I don't train their parents."

"Oh."

"Generally speaking, people hire nannies because they have obligations that take them away from their children for specified periods of time," she went on. "Often, quite substantial periods of time. That leaves a great deal of the childcare in my hands, and that's what I've been trained to handle."

"Right." He still didn't entirely see the problem here. "I understand that. I'm not asking you to give me formal lessons or anything. My plan is just to observe you and figure out how you handle the boys so well." He offered a hopeful smile. "I learned my best marketing techniques by watching top-notch salesmen, and I'm confident I can do the same thing here. If I'm confused about something and have a question, I'll ask. Otherwise, you can just look at me as a sort of apprentice—a really inexperienced one. I'll hang around, carry things and generally make myself useful."

His explanation didn't seem to help. Her frown deepened. "It's not what I do," she repeated, a hint of desperation in her voice. "I accepted this job with a certain…expectation…of what my duties would be."

"I understand that. But this isn't exactly a typical situation, is it? Like you pointed out, you'll only be here for the summer. Then I'm going to need to take the reins again. And there's the whole issue of the boys—Tuck especially—getting too attached to you. If I'm around all the time, too, maybe that wouldn't be so much of a problem."

She nodded, her hazel eyes worried. "I do see your point. But—"

"Elise." He leaned forward in his seat, intending to explain that he'd stay out of the way. That he wouldn't cause trouble or do anything to make her uncomfortable.

She immediately scooted backward, carefully maintaining her distance. He frowned and settled back in his chair, noting how the tension in her shoulders eased when he moved away.

He was too late with his promises. That ship had already sailed.

He made Elise Cooper very uncomfortable.

Which meant he'd messed up even worse than he thought, and he was probably about one more blunder away from watching her walk out the door. He didn't like to think about what would happen to the twins if she did. They were already doing so much better.

He needed to prove he wasn't a threat—and the only way to do that was to swallow what was left of his pride and be honest about how desperate he really was.

And why.

It took him a few seconds. He didn't much like the idea of showing this woman the worst of himself. But he understood people well enough to know that he didn't have much choice.

"Look." He drew in a deep breath. "Maybe it'll help if I explain a few things. May I?"

"Of course."

"My sister had some addiction problems, and she and I weren't always on the best of terms. But before she died, she put it in writing that she wanted me to be the twins' guardian. Because—for some reason—she trusted me." He swallowed, but the lump in his throat was stubborn. "Over the years, I'd done a lot of preaching at her about good choices and family and all that, so she had her reasons to think I'd be man enough to step up to the plate. But before you came— the day you came for your interview, actually— I asked Logan if he'd consider taking the boys."

She blinked a few times, and that faint line formed on her forehead again. "You were considering relinquishing custody?"

"Yeah. I don't like admitting it, but it's the truth. Things were going really bad, and they'd been getting worse by the day. I was on the verge of giving up, and believe it or not, Elise, giving up isn't something I tend to do."

"Oh, I believe it." There was no mistaking the sincerity in her voice, but he wasn't sure she meant it as a compliment.

"In all fairness, I didn't have the best example of fatherhood to fall back on. My dad's addiction was gambling, not drugs, but when it came to parenting, he was as irresponsible as an alley cat. When I was a kid, my life was—" He discarded four adjectives before he decided on one that didn't come close to covering the reality. "Hard."

"I see," she murmured.

He doubted she did. He was pretty certain she had no idea of the level of hard he was talking about.

He hoped not, anyway.

"I had to look after myself. My dad remarried a few times, but the kind of woman who fell for my father…let's just say they weren't the type to embrace being a stepmother. I did what I had to do to get by. I stole. I conned people, and I never felt guilty about it. And then I met Ruby." In spite of the seriousness of this conversation, he smiled. He always did when he thought about his foster mom. "Ruby has three antidotes to whatever problems life throws at her—prayer, honesty and hard work. I learned how to live a good life by watching her. You know the most important lesson she taught me?"

Elise raised one eyebrow.

"To never give up on people. Ruby sure didn't. Pretty much everybody had given up on us kids by the time we got to her house, but not her. She stuck with us, no matter how tough we made things for her. And believe me, we made things plenty tough before she got us turned around."

"She sounds like a wonderful woman." The

wariness in Elise's eyes had been replaced by interest. This conversation was working.

"She is. You'll find out just how wonderful for yourself before long. She's been champing at the bit to meet you. Unless I miss my guess, she'll insist on having us over for supper pretty soon. Before you leave, she'll know everything from your favorite food to your shoe size, and your name will be on the prayer list she keeps in her Bible. And you might as well answer her questions because like I told you, Ruby's not the kind who gives up. And neither am I. That's the reason I've done all right in sales, because I just won't give up. Except when it came to the most important responsibilities I've ever been given in my life. I gave up on my sister because I got frustrated with her relapses. And I almost gave up on the twins because they were climbing the walls, and I was clueless about how to help them. Then you showed up. And it was like God was showing me that this was doable. That I could learn how to take care of them."

Uneasiness clouded back into her eyes. "Oh, Ryder," she began, shaking her head. "I don't know."

"You know how to manage the boys. And if you can do it, then I have to believe—or at least hope—that I can learn how to do it, too." He leaned forward, very slightly. This time she didn't move away. "I don't want to give up on them, and I want to learn how to be the best dad I can be. But I'm going to need your help."

She looked at him, her face crinkled with worry. Finally, she sighed.

"All right," she said. "I'll do my best. But," she went on in a firmer voice. "If you truly want to learn from me, then that means following my instructions even when you think you have a better idea. I'm not going to be able to teach you very much—or help the boys—if you don't."

"Agreed." Relieved, he scooped up his phone and stood. A good salesman always knew when to leave. He didn't want to linger long enough for her to start having second thoughts.

"And there's one more thing."

Uh-oh. "What's that?"

She rose to her feet and fastened him with a stern eye. "You have to give me your word that you'll keep things strictly professional."

"Absolutely. No more flowers, and I'll cancel the ten-pound box of chocolates I ordered." He almost laughed at her horrified expression. "Kidding, Elise. Only kidding."

She didn't smile. "I'm not. We'll be spending quite a lot of time together, and the only way that'll work is if we maintain appropriate boundaries."

Yeah, Ryder thought grimly. Jerk Guy—whoever he was—must have been a real piece of work.

"You have my word." He stuck out his hand. "Thank you, Elise. I appreciate this." Her fingers felt small and delicate in his grip, but he gave her his best I-mean-business handshake.

Even so, for some reason—gratitude, he supposed—he found himself reluctant to let her hand go. But he managed it. He'd struck a deal, and he was determined to keep it.

He smiled. "I'll see myself out."

As he turned to shut the door, she was just settling back into her chair. Her face was still puckered with worry as she lifted her teacup to her mouth. She had one leg tucked up underneath herself, and the warm glow of the lamp beside her brought golden glints out in her hair.

He felt a sharp pang of longing.

It really would have been nice to spend an hour or two in this quiet room in the evenings. Talking about what they were reading, maybe. Or something funny the twins had said. He didn't see the harm in that.

But Elise had made it very clear that she was the boys' nanny, not his friend. It had taken every skill he possessed to pull this deal out of the fire. He might not be able to do that a second time. Besides, he'd given her his word, and he was going to keep it. Period.

"Enjoy your book," he said. "And your tea. Good night."

"Good night, Ryder."

He started across the yard to a house that looked a lot colder and darker after Elise's cozy domain. He paused on the back steps, casting one last wistful look at the cottage's glowing windows.

Then he went inside and shut the door.

Chapter Six

Early the next morning, Elise sat at the kitchen table in the little cottage, her phone pressed against her ear and her eyes squeezed shut. This way it seemed as if Nanny Bev was sitting beside her, instead of an ocean away in London. She could almost smell the scent of lemons.

"So?" she asked. "What do you think about this whole training-the-parent idea?"

Her old nanny's familiar chuckle rippled through the phone. "I think it's quite commendable that this Mr. Montgomery wants to learn how to care for his nephews. Usually, you know, we have the opposite problem with parents."

"That's true, I suppose. But I've no idea how to go about this."

"I expect you'll figure it out. You're quite a clever girl. Anyway, that's not really what's bothering you. You mustn't paint a new wall with an old brush, love. This fellow doesn't sound a bit like that Mr. Bartley who gave you such difficulty. And remember, your father had nothing at all to do with this job offer, so it's hardly the same sort of thing."

"Not a setup, you mean." Elise still couldn't believe she'd fallen for James Bartley's *I'm just a poor single dad who needs your help* routine. But she had—hook, line and sinker. He'd had little trouble persuading her to bend her rules about spending her free time with an employer.

Their little scratch suppers and movie-watching on the couch had all seemed harmless at the time—even rather sweet. In fact, she'd been right on the brink of falling in love. Until she'd discovered the charming Bartley had been promised a plum promotion in her father's company—assuming, of course, that he could convince Elise to marry him.

She'd discovered that fact thanks to Bartley's smirking ex-wife—ten minutes before Bartley proposed in front of all his friends. She still cringed at the memory.

"No," she assured Nanny Bev now. "Dad would never approve of Ryder. He doesn't come from the right sort of family." Another firm mark in her new employer's favor. "Not to mention he foiled Dad's plan to force me home for the summer."

"I expect you're right." Nanny Bev tsked her

tongue. "Such a shame, really, this ongoing tiff between you and your father. I never approve of such squabbles in families."

"Hardly avoidable in this case. The only way my father's going to be happy is if I allow him to control my life. And that's not going to happen."

"Of course not. You've a mind of your own and a healthy dash of Mr. Cooper's own stubbornness, which is a nice bit of poetic justice. It's my prayer that one day you and your father will be able to settle your differences and get along. He means well—"

Elise sighed. "Nanny Bev—"

"Don't interrupt when someone else is speaking. It's rude." The tart reminder came crisply across the miles, and Elise's mouth curved upward. Nanny Bev never changed. It was one of the most comforting things about her.

"I apologize," Elise murmured.

"Accepted. As I was saying, I believe your father means well. All these outlandish schemes are simply his extraordinarily clumsy way of showing that he wants the best for you. One can hardly fault any parent for that."

Her mind slipped to Ryder, and his bumbling attempts to look after the little boys in his charge.

"Maybe. But in my father's case, clumsy is an understatement."

"Perhaps," Nanny Bev conceded. "And I'm not

saying I approve of his methods. Only that sometimes we must look at people's hearts rather than
their mistakes. Now, love, I'm afraid I must go.
It's nearly lunchtime, and we're having a special
send-off today for my friend Marge."

"Marge is leaving?" Marge Robinson was
Nanny Bev's dearest buddy at the retirement
home. "I'm so sorry. You'll miss her terribly,
won't you?"

"Yes, indeed. Of course, at my age, one sadly
does become accustomed to friends' departures."

Elise frowned. "But Marge didn't—she hasn't—"

"Died? Oh, no. She's in the pink of health.
She's simply moving to less expensive accommodations. They're raising the prices again here,
starting next month."

Raising the prices? Again? Elise's heart fell.
She had to scrimp to make her part of the pay-
ments as it was, and Nanny Bev was on a fixed
income. "How much?"

"I can't recall the precise figure, but apparently it's quite a substantial increase. I'm planning to ring my solicitor this afternoon and have
him check my finances to see if I'll be able to
remain myself. I do hope so. I've seen enough of
these places over the years to know that this es-
tablishment is one of the best available. But don't
worry about me, love. This isn't the first time

costs have gone up, but so far the Good Lord's always worked it out just fine."

"That's true." Elise only wished He'd tip her off about exactly how He was planning to do that.

She needed to know details, but she dared not ask any more questions. The topic of finances was one she studiously avoided with Nanny Bev. Ever since the retirement home's last increase, when the older woman had worried aloud that she wouldn't be able to afford to remain in Glen Haven, Elise had been making up the difference. She remitted the amount of money to Nanny's solicitor each month, and the kindhearted elderly attorney quietly applied it to the bill. He'd vaguely explained it to Nanny Bev as an ongoing "benevolence" available to her because of her lifetime of caretaking. To Elise's relief, the older woman had accepted the anonymous windfall happily, calling it an answer to prayer.

It was certainly an answer to Elise's prayers. She'd been delighted to have an opportunity to do something kind for the woman who'd practically raised her—and inspired her to begin her own nannying career.

But if the price was going up again…and substantially…that was going to be a problem. There simply wasn't that much cushion in Elise's budget. She'd call the lawyer herself and see what he knew about the situation.

"I'd best let you go, Nanny Bev. You won't want to miss saying goodbye to Marge."

"Yes, and you'll be needing to get to work! Call again when you can. And don't fret yourself over this arrangement you've made with your Mr. Montgomery. I feel quite certain you're up to the task. No doubt you'll have him in fine shape by the end of the summer."

She wasn't so sure, but right now she had other things to worry about. "Well, we'll see, I suppose. Love you, Nanny Bev."

"And I you, my dear."

The minute she disconnected the call, Elise placed a second one, this time to Nanny Bev's lawyer. Her brief conversation with Mr. Farnsworth wasn't reassuring. Sure enough, the increase was more than Elise could manage.

When she broke that news to the attorney, he cleared his throat. "Forgive me if I'm overstepping, but your father's rather wealthy, isn't he? And Beverly was in his service for quite some time. You don't suppose—"

"No." Her father wouldn't help. He'd fired Nanny Bev years ago after a decade of faithful service—with no warning and no explanation.

"Pity." Farnsworth sighed. "In that case, I suppose the best thing is to see if more affordable accommodations can be found. Will you be able to assist with that?"

"I'll try. Of course, it's difficult to manage such things long-distance. I don't think I'll be able to pay for more than a month or so at the higher price, but that gives us a little time to find a solution."

After ending the call, Elise sat at the table, chin in hand, thinking hard. Then she glanced at the slim watch on her wrist—a gift from Nanny Bev when she'd finished her nanny training—and rose to her feet.

She'd best report to work, and hope Nanny Bev was right, that she could, in fact, figure out how to teach Ryder Montgomery how to manage his nephews in just a few short weeks. Because now she needed this job more than ever.

Ryder sat at the kitchen table beside the twins, inhaling the aroma of brewing coffee with desperate appreciation. Mornings with the twins started at the crack of dawn, usually with some sort of free-for-all. Since he was also staying up late trying to get some work done, he was tired before the day even got started.

He looked it, too. He'd thrown on khaki shorts and a white T-shirt this morning. The clothes were wrinkled, but relatively clean. He hadn't shaved, though, and his brief glance into the mirror had revealed a guy with some serious bags under his eyes.

Elise, on the other hand, looked crisply professional in pressed slacks and a yellow blouse, and—except for one new worried line across her brow—completely calm.

She didn't look happy. More resigned. But she was still here, and at this point, he'd take what he could get.

She'd also made coffee, so right now she was his favorite person on the planet.

"Lesson one, managing meals. Offer limited choices," she murmured as she passed him on the way to the refrigerator. "All appropriate ones. That's the secret." She lifted her voice. "Benji? Tucker? Would you prefer your eggs scrambled or boiled this morning?"

The twins considered. "Scwambled," Benji announced.

"With cheese mixed in," Tucker added.

"Very well." Elise took the eggs out of the refrigerator, along with some butter and milk and a package of grated cheddar cheese. "Red or green apple slices?"

"Red," Benji said.

"Green," Tucker objected with a scowl.

The two boys glared at each other. Ryder's gut tightened, but Elise didn't blink. "Benji spoke first, so we will have red for breakfast. But," she added smoothly as Benji stuck out a triumphant tongue at his brother, "we'll have green apple slices with our lunch. Perhaps your uncle will slice the apple for us?"

"Sure." Ryder reluctantly set down his untasted coffee before scooping a red apple out of the wooden bowl on the table. He crossed to the sink, beside Elise, who stood at the stove melting a pat of butter in a small saucepan.

"Your turn," she murmured under her breath.

"What?"

"They'll need something to drink."

"Oh, right." He turned on the faucet and rinsed the apple. "Guys? What do you want to drink?"

He heard Elise's soft cluck of disapproval just as he realized his mistake.

"Coke!" the boys chorused gleefully. Soda had been their go-to drink choice since arrival.

"Uh, we don't have any Coke. Orange juice or milk?"

"Coffee!" Benji reached for the still-steaming mug Ryder had left behind.

Everything morphed into slow motion. Ryder lunged for the table just as Benji's fingers made contact with the mug's handle.

A split second later, Benji was howling in the bathroom while Elise held his reddened fingers under a running stream of cold water. Ryder was on his hands and knees under the table, cleaning up spilled coffee and bits of broken mug.

Tucker kicked his small bare feet dangerously close to Ryder's head. "I'm hungry," he whined.

"I know, buddy. Hang on for a minute, and we'll get you some food."

"I'm hungry *now*." The child started to slide off his chair, his feet aimed at a muddy pool of coffee and mug shards.

Ryder dropped the wad of paper towels and grabbed for Tucker. He caught the boy in mid-slide, his bare toes dangling a scant inch away from the danger zone.

"Better wait until I get this cleaned up. Come on," he said, swinging the child up into his arms. "Let's go see how your brother's doing."

Tucker cocked his head, listening to the yelling coming from the hall bathroom. "Not so good," he said solemnly.

They found Elise patting Benji's scarlet fingers dry with a clean towel. "It's all right," she said comfortingly. "I'll put a smear of aloe gel on, and you'll be just fine."

"It hurts!" Benji sobbed.

"I'm sure it does." Elise tapped the child's nose gently. "But it'll feel better soon. And I don't suppose you'll go grabbing for hot coffee again, will you?"

The boy snuffled. "Nope."

As Elise reached for the door of the medicine cabinet, she caught sight of Ryder standing in the

Laurel Blount 121

doorway, Tucker in his arms. "Oh, dear. Do we have another casualty?"

"No, but it was a near miss. Do you suppose you could keep an eye on the twins while I finish cleaning the kitchen?"

"Certainly. Boys, let's go upstairs and get you dressed. Then you can come to my house for breakfast while your uncle cleans up."

"Okay!" The boys' faces lit up, even Benji's tear-stained one. They'd been fascinated by Elise's cottage since day one, and obviously they were thrilled with the prospect of another visit.

Remembering how he'd felt last night, Ryder couldn't exactly blame them.

He put Tucker down and stepped back from the doorway as Elise led Benji out of the bathroom.

"Thanks," he murmured as she passed. "This shouldn't take long, and I'll be ready to *help* some more." He put a wry spin on the word, and she shot him a look he was coming to recognize—mingled alarm and amusement.

"Take your time. In fact, you might as well go ahead and get a shower, or—" she paused, looking flustered, "—whatever you need to do to get ready for the day."

He glanced down at his rumpled outfit. Not exactly magazine-cover-worthy, but he'd figured it was good enough for chasing twins around a yard. "Are we going someplace?"

"To the library," Elise said. "It's time for the boys to make amends so they won't be banned for the rest of the summer."

"Oh." In that case, yeah, he'd better spruce up. "Okay. Give me about twenty minutes."

She nodded as she led the boys upstairs.

It was more like half an hour before Ryder knocked on Elise's door. That coffee had spread everywhere, and he'd gone over the floor three times, checking for tiny slivers of mug. Then he'd taken time to shave because Mrs. Bishop didn't seem like the sort of woman who'd find scruff attractive.

Elise opened the door, but to his surprise, instead of inviting him in, she stepped out on the porch.

"Finish your breakfast, boys," she called cheerfully over her shoulder. "And put your plates in the sink. We're leaving in ten minutes." Then she turned back to Ryder, her face shifting into seriousness. "All right," she said in a low voice. "We don't have very long, so we'd best get a few things straight. If you truly want me to teach you, then you really must pay attention to what I tell you."

Ryder felt stung. "Yeah. Sorry about the drink thing. It was just…early, and I was operating on a few hours of sleep and no coffee."

He could see Elise getting a firmer grip on her

patience. "I see. But I'd just explained the procedure not five minutes before. Listening is the first key to success."

Ryder fought hard to keep his mouth in a straight line. Hearing these old-fashioned statements coming out of Elise's mouth always made him want to chuckle. "I'll listen more closely from now on. I promise."

Elise appeared unconvinced, but she nodded. "Good."

On the way out the door, Ryder impulsively grabbed the large arrangement of flowers. Elise looked at it askance as he crowded it into the space between the front seats. Tight fit, but it stood a much better chance of survival up here than it would in the back with the boys.

"Since you don't want this, I figured I'd offer it to Mrs. Bishop," he explained.

"Oh." Elise looked skeptical, but she shrugged. "I suppose it can't hurt."

Happily, Mrs. Bishop proved to be a bigger fan of oversize flower arrangements. The librarian darted appreciative glances at the blooms gracing her circulation desk as Elise explained the purpose of their visit.

However, even the flowers apparently didn't make up for her damaged books. She listened to the boys' carefully rehearsed apologies with a stern face.

"I'm glad to hear you're sorry," she said, tsking her tongue. "Treating valuable library materials in such a manner—not to mention the damage you might have done to my eye. Your apology is accepted, and you may visit the library and check out books again, as long as you're very careful with them. However—" she firmed up her mouth "—I'm afraid story time is still off-limits."

Ryder threw Elise an *I told you so* look. He'd warned her Mrs. Bishop wouldn't be easy to charm.

Elise's expression remained serene.

"In addition to their apology, the twins would like to offer their services here," she said. "To make up for the expenses they caused. Surely there's some task they could help you with."

The librarian's expression shifted into horror so fast it was comical. Forgiving the twins was one thing. Having them "helping" in her precious library was obviously quite another. Ryder covered his chuckle with a well-timed cough.

"I don't think..."

"The library has such lovely grounds," Elise interjected smoothly. "Perhaps some weed pulling and stick removal might be helpful. Under my close supervision, of course."

The boys exchanged an unhappy look, and Mrs. Bishop didn't seem to like the idea all that much either.

"I'm not sure," she hedged. "We employ a service for lawn maintenance, and we have a custodian who attends to small outdoor tasks."

"I noticed him working outside when we drove up," Elise said. "He's rather elderly, isn't he? I'm sure he'd appreciate some help. The boys and I will walk outside and ask him what little jobs they might do."

Before Mrs. Bishop could object, Elise had shepherded the twins out the door. The librarian looked bewildered, and Ryder smothered a smile.

If she hadn't decided to become a nanny, Elise could have had a stellar career in sales.

Mrs. Bishop cleared her throat and busied herself arranging pads and pencils on the circulation desk. "Miss Cooper seems very competent. You were blessed to find such a good caretaker for the twins. Especially," she added, "given the… circumstances."

He couldn't argue with that. "Definitely."

The librarian looked thoughtful. "Perhaps I should ask her for some tips for managing my grandchildren. They're delightful children, but you know…rather active." The older woman darted another admiring look at the large bouquet. "Thank you for the flowers. Such a generous gesture. I imagine they were quite expensive."

Ryder's eyes narrowed. Something in Mrs. Bishop's tone stirred his instincts. "I'm glad you like them, and please don't worry about the cost. I worked out a deal with the florist."

"I'm sure you did," Mrs. Bishop said dryly. "You always were good at that sort of thing. I've lost track of the fines you've renegotiated over the years." She sighed. "I wish I had that skill. There are so many things the library could use."

Ryder glanced around, noting the threadbare carpet and the cumbersome, outdated computer monitors at the technology stations. He remembered how upset Mrs. Bishop had been about the damage to the books the boys had thrown. At the time, he'd been too distracted by the twins' behavior to notice all the little tells, but now things clicked into place.

This was about money, he realized. This small-town library was hurting for cash.

Confidence surged up in him. Finally, something he understood. Maybe he floundered with kid care, but he was an expert when it came to cash shortages.

Having them—and solving them.

He could redeem himself with Elise for all his recent goof-ups and make sure the twins were welcomed here with open arms from now on.

"Mrs. Bishop?" Ryder smiled and leaned across the scuffed-up wooden desk. "You and I should talk."

Chapter Seven

Fixing the library's cash flow problem took Ryder exactly fifteen minutes and three phone calls. By the time Elise and the twins came back inside, Mrs. Bishop's face was beaming with excitement, and she was scribbling her wish list down on a legal pad.

"I just can't thank you enough," she said for the tenth time. "You've no idea what a difference this is going to make!"

"I'm glad I could help."

He really was. There was a satisfaction in seeing the crusty librarian's face relaxed into an astonished joy just because he'd phoned in a few favors. It'd been so simple, too. His friends were happy to make small—to them, anyway—donations to help a struggling library, particularly if it put Ryder Montgomery in their debt.

"Mrs. Bishop?" Elise approached the circulation desk with the boys. She glanced between them, obviously curious about what was going on. "We've spoken to the custodian and made plans for Tucker and Benji to come back tomorrow morning and help tidy up the flower beds. According to Mr. Aldridge, that will save him about two hours' work, which should cover the cost of the damaged books."

"Don't worry about that," Mrs. Bishop said with a smile. "As it happens, restitution won't be necessary. Their generous uncle has handled everything."

The twins looked at each other. They grinned, and Ryder's heart sank.

"I'm sorry." Elise frowned. "I don't understand. I thought we agreed the boys needed to make amends for their misbehavior themselves."

"Right," Ryder assured her hastily. "And the boys can still do that. Can't they, Mrs. Bishop?"

"Whatever you like," the librarian agreed vaguely. "But as I said, it truly isn't necessary. I shouldn't have been so…unyielding about this matter. I've been under a great deal of pressure lately, and I'm afraid it's made me rather cranky." She turned eagerly back to Ryder. "And your friend's company has agreed to donate a dozen new computers? A dozen? And your other friend is going to replace *all* the carpeting?"

"Yes," Ryder confirmed, keeping a wary eye

on Elise's face. "The bathroom linoleum, too. And as soon as you finish that wish list, Atlanta Media will provide the funds for those items as well."

To his astonishment, Mrs. Bishop disregarded her own strict rules and clapped her hands, earning surprised looks from the library patrons. "Oh, it's going to make such a difference! Boys, forget what I said about story time. You're most welcome to attend."

Judging from the new warmth in her voice, the twins could have thrown every book in the library without Mrs. Bishop so much as raising an eyebrow. He caught the boys sharing another sidelong look, and he suspected that truth had filtered into their little brains as well.

Oh, brother. He could feel this nicely fixed situation sliding sideways, and he had no idea how to stop it. But the first logical step was to get them out of the library so he could explain this to Elise.

She didn't look at all happy.

"I'll continue to work on this list," the librarian promised fervently. "And I promise you, every single item will be an absolute necessity. I won't waste a penny of this windfall you've arranged."

"I'm sure you won't. Mrs. Bishop, we're supposed to go up to Ruby's for lunch today, so we're going to have to get going."

"Oh! Of course." She took one of Ryder's hands in both of hers. "Thank you. Thank you so very much. And you tell Ruby that I knew. I always knew—in spite of that regrettable afternoon when you stuck your chewing gum between the pages of *The Old Man and the Sea*—that one day you'd learn to appreciate books."

It was obviously her highest compliment, so Ryder offered her a stiff smile. As they turned to leave, he heard the librarian muttering delightedly.

"Three phone calls. He made three phone calls, and everything's fixed. I simply can't comprehend it."

The minute they were outside, the twins ran ahead down the sidewalk toward the small parking area.

"Did you write her a check?" Elise asked quietly when the boys were safely out of earshot. "That wasn't the plan."

"I didn't," he hastened to assure her. "I didn't give her a penny. I just made a few phone calls, that's all, to people in a position to give the library some assistance. And it needs it. Surely you can see that. The whole place is shabby, and according to Mrs. Bishop, their annual budget's a joke."

"Oh, yes. I see, all right."

His heart sank at her exasperated tone. "You're mad."

"No." Elise made the correction crisply. "I'm confused. I thought we had an agreement."

"We did. We do."

"Apparently not. An agreement implies that both parties will stick to the plan."

"We are. You heard Mrs. Bishop. The boys can still come and do their chores here to make up for what they did."

"I also heard her say—twice—that they didn't have to, thanks to you. And they heard that as well." Elise stopped on the sidewalk and sighed. "Which—and I really shouldn't have to point this out—completely negates the lesson I was trying to teach."

Ryder glanced at the boys. They were paying them no attention. They'd found an earthworm in some freshly turned dirt by the sidewalk and were poking him gently with a leaf.

"I'm sorry. I wasn't trying to mess up your plan. It's just…did you see the carpet in there? It's worn all the way through in several places. And those computers—" Ryder shook his head. He couldn't even start to describe those. They were so old and clunky they'd make Torey weep. "The library truly needs the help."

"Yes, it does. And from the look of it, it's needed help for quite some time. And yet you were only motivated to get involved now." She tilted her head. "Why is that?" When he didn't answer immediately, she nodded. "Because this really isn't about helping the library, is it? It's exactly the same as the bracelet. This is about buying the twins' way out of trouble."

Ryder started to argue, then stopped. "Okay," he conceded. "Maybe—just maybe—there's a little truth in that."

Elise made a skeptical noise. If she weren't so prim and proper, he'd have called it a raspberry. "Maybe?"

"Okay, probably. But not buying their way out of trouble. Just…easing their way back into Mrs. Bishop's good graces. And making sure she isn't quite so easy to make mad the next time. What's wrong with that?"

She sighed. "You're teaching them that money's the solution to every problem. It isn't."

"Says someone who's never had to try solving problems without it." The words came out more sharply than he meant them to, and she flinched. "I'm sorry," he said quickly. "But trust me. Sometimes money makes things much easier."

"Easier, maybe. Better? I'm not so sure." She glanced at her watch. "I'd hate to keep Mrs. Sawyer waiting, and it's nearly twelve. Maybe we'd better continue this discussion later."

"Elise—"

But she was already pulling a package of hand

wipes out of her purse and advancing down the sidewalk toward the twins. "Wipe your hands, boys. Yes, he *is* a lovely worm, Benji, but he'll be much happier in the dirt than in your pocket. Yes, I'm quite sure."

Ryder watched her take the squirming worm from Benji's reluctant fingers and place it gently on the ground. She regarded it with a curled lip and a little shudder.

"Ugh," he heard her whisper. Then a second later she was briskly herding the boys toward the car, wiping her own fingers as she went.

He followed along behind, casting a sympathetic look at the rejected worm as he passed.

"I know how you feel, buddy," he muttered. "She's not too crazy about me right now either."

On the ride up the winding mountain road to Ruby's, Elise kept her expression pleasant and tried her best to appreciate the pretty summer foliage rolling past the car window.

She shouldn't have been quite so snippy back at the library. She'd just been really frustrated. Ryder had rolled over her good, old-fashioned lesson about consequences like a charming eighteen-wheeler.

But she'd certainly had such issues with employers before, and she'd always handled them professionally. After all, when it came down to it, all the decisions relating to the children in her charge belonged to their parents. No nanny worth her salt could afford to forget that.

She didn't know why Ryder Montgomery got under her skin so often. It was really quite puzzling.

One thing was for sure. She'd have to find some way to politely convince him to give up on this whole "teach me how to parent" idea. It obviously wasn't going to work. If he'd leave her in peace, she was confident she could get the boys' worst behaviors well under control and have them ready for pre-K in the fall.

If Ryder kept "helping," she wasn't so sure that would happen.

For now, though, she'd put the entire issue out of her mind. She was already nervous about meeting this Ruby Sawyer she'd heard so much about. She'd like to make a good impression, and she needed her wits about her.

A few minutes later, Ryder pulled into the yard of a white farmhouse, bathed in the glow of the noon sun. Elise surveyed Ruby's home with interest—and approval. It had a peaceful charm she instinctively liked. This was a house designed to shelter and welcome loved ones, not impress strangers.

Apparently she wasn't the only one who liked it. The minute the twins were freed from their car seats, they barreled toward the porch and vanished inside, the screen door slapping shut behind them.

Elise frowned and hurried toward the house. The twins were supposed to be under her supervision. So much for making a good first impression.

"Elise?" Ryder called after her. "Wait a second."

She threw an uncertain glance toward the farmhouse. "I'd better get inside, don't you think? The boys—"

"They'll be fine with Ruby for a minute. Look, I'm really sorry for upsetting you. It wasn't my intention to sidetrack the lesson you were trying to teach the boys. I just saw an opportunity to smooth things over and do some good for the library." He gave her a hopeful smile. "And it wasn't a complete disaster. Did you see Mrs. Bishop's face? I haven't seen her smile like that since…well, ever. And we'll take the boys over to help the custodian on Tuesday just as planned, and we'll make sure they sweat out the cost of those books. Okay?"

We.

"Ryder, I really don't think—"

"Y'all planning to eat lunch out here?"

Startled, Elise looked toward the farmhouse. A short, spare-framed woman with grizzled gray hair stood at the front door. As their eyes met, a smile lit up her wrinkled face, and she beckoned with one hand.

"Come on in! Lunch is ready."

Elise smiled back. So this was Ruby Sawyer.

Thanks to her father's social position, she'd been introduced to many remarkable people over the years. They were often surprisingly ordinary to look at.

Ruby was no exception.

This woman was plain, and her shabby clothes were two decades out of fashion. But when she looked at Ryder, her hazel eyes shone with such motherly affection that for a minute, she was beautiful.

Ryder must have thought so too. As soon as he was close enough, he leaned down and kissed her cheek. "Ruby, you get prettier every time I see you."

Ruby swatted him. "Go tell your fibs to somebody else." But she was still smiling when she turned to Elise.

"So you're the nanny I've heard so much about."

"I've heard a great deal about you, too. It's a pleasure to meet you." Elise offered a hand.

"Nope." Ruby stepped forward, enveloping Elise in a strong hug. "I ain't just shaking hands with you, honey. Not after what you've done for my family. We've been real worried about those twins, but couldn't none of us get them straightened out. Not even me, and I've dealt with plenty of troublesome young'uns over the years." She cut a teasing look at Ryder. "Present company included. But you've turned out to be just what those boys needed."

Ruby stepped back, her bony fingers still gripping Elise's arms and gave her a thorough once-over. "Well, aren't you a pretty thing? That's something I haven't heard about. Of course, nowadays, Logan's got no eyes for any woman but his Charlotte. But I'm kinda surprised Ryder here didn't mention it." She cast a measuring look at her foster son, who—to Elise's amusement—colored like a schoolboy.

"Cut it out, Ruby. You're embarrassing Elise," he said.

"Looks more like I'm embarrassing you." His mother's eyes twinkled. "Come on in. The boys are washing up." Looping one arm cozily around Elise's waist, Ruby drew her into the house.

The inside of Ruby's home was as welcoming as the outside. It was spotlessly clean, a little threadbare, and arranged with comfort in mind. The kitchen's outdated appliances and worn linoleum sported a shine that came—Elise was sure—from Ruby's elbow grease. The window above the sink was cracked open, and a mountain breeze ruffled the red-checkered curtains, wafting the homey aromas of fried chicken and fresh bread around the kitchen.

The twins were already seated at the table. They glanced up as the adults approached, their faces guilty. A jam jar was pulled close to their plates, and a suspicious stickiness was smeared around their mouths.

Ruby spoke before Elise could. "Got into my jam, did you? You use a spoon or your fingers?"

"Spoon," Benji said.

Ruby chuckled. "That's an improvement, I reckon. Have a seat," she invited Elise. "Let's eat before everything gets cold."

Ruby turned out to be an exceptional cook. Even the twins—who weren't always cooperative when it came to food—ate happily.

"See? These here are our kinda biscuits." Tucker held a gravy-laden example aloft. He turned to Ruby. "Nanny Elise thinks biscuits are cookies."

"Maybe they are where she comes from. We don't make fun of folks who talk different from us. That just makes 'em more interesting. Put that biscuit down on your plate before you get gravy everywhere."

When the child obeyed her instruction promptly, Ruby lifted one skimpy eyebrow. "They *are* doing better," she murmured to Elise. "Time was, anything I told that child to do, he'd do the opposite, just to spite me. Seems like you know your business."

"From what I hear, so do you, Mrs. Sawyer."

"Call me Ruby." The older woman smiled. "And you shouldn't believe everything my kids tell you. They give me more credit than I deserve. Have some more coleslaw, honey. It's my own special recipe."

"It's delicious." Elise allowed another heaping spoonful of the slaw to be added to her already laden plate.

She doubted Ruby's foster kids were exaggerating their praise of their mom. This mountain woman reminded Elise strongly of Nanny Bev. She had a different accent, but the same kind look, the same air of loving authority.

She also had the same habit of sneaking personal questions into a conversation. As the meal progressed, Elise found herself telling Ruby all sorts of details about her job history, her education and her family life—or lack thereof.

"You're an only child? Good thing I didn't let my whole crew come today, then. They're a lot to take, even when you're used to 'em. When everybody's here, you can't hardly get a word in edgewise. 'Specially since Maggie and Logan have each married and started families of their own. You ain't married, are you, honey? Got some fellow waiting for you back up in Virginia?"

"Ruby!" Ryder shot Elise a horrified look.

Elise fought a smile. "I'm afraid not."

"Well, ain't that a shame?" Ruby murmured—not sounding as if she thought it was a shame at all. In fact, she sounded oddly pleased. "Sounds like a lonely life, if you ask me. I spend a good deal of time praying for my single kids, 'specially Ryder here. Now that the twins have come to live with him, he don't have much time to date. I reckon the Good Lord will just have to drop the right woman on his doorstep." She smiled.

"Can we change the subject?" Ryder asked desperately.

His foster mother sent him an innocent look over her glass of iced tea. "Sure." She pushed her chair back and stood. "Tell you what, son. You and these boys clear the table while I show Elise the quilt I'm making."

"A quilt?" Elise put her napkin beside her plate. "I love quilts!"

Ruby beamed. "Good! Now, mind you, I'm no great shakes at making 'em. My daughter-in-law's been teaching me. She can sew just about anything, Charlotte can. She helped me make Logan's, and now I'm working on Ryder's all by my lonesome."

"I'd love to see it."

"I'm not sure this is such a good idea," Ryder

interjected, but Ruby waved him off with an age-spotted hand.

"Whyever not? You heard Elise here. She likes quilts. Now get busy and scrape off them dishes. We'll be back in time to help with the washing up."

Ryder didn't look happy, but he didn't protest. That was another thing Ruby and Nanny Bev had in common, Elise thought as she followed the older woman into the hallway. It never did any good to argue with them.

In a small, tidy bedroom, Ruby opened an old wardrobe and took out a bundle of fabric. She laid the pieces gently across the bed.

"It ain't finished," she explained. "I've got the squares pieced, and now I'm hand-sewing them together. But if I lay them out like so, you can get a good idea of what it's gonna look like."

"It's beautiful."

It was. The quilt, featuring calming shades of green and blue, was made up of at least a hundred tiny squares, pieced into blocks. The scraps were arranged so that the colors went from pale in one corner of the quilt to deep and intense on the opposite end.

Ruby traced the color change with one gnarled finger. "See how it brightens up, like? I come up with the idea myself, but Charlotte says other folks have done it, too. She says it's called gradated colors, or some such thing. I probably ain't got the word just right."

"Whatever it's called, it's a lovely effect."

Ruby tilted her head, studying her creation. "I think it's turning out real well. It's a memory quilt, you know."

"A memory quilt?"

"That's right. Every one of them squares comes from a shirt Ryder wore, and each one's got a memory attached to it. Like this one here." She put her finger on a light blue square in the middle of the piece. "Wore that 'un to his very first job interview down at the hardware store when he was fifteen years old. Got the job, too."

"I'm sure he did."

"Old Arty Stevens still says Ryder was the best worker he ever had. Ran circles around them other teenaged boys. Got himself a raise the first week. Can't everybody say that—'specially not with Arty. That man's a skinflint if there ever was one. But he knew what he had in Ryder, and he wanted to keep him long as he could. And this one here—" Ruby indicated a deep green square close to the brightest corner "—this here's the shirt he wore to Logan and Charlotte's wedding last fall. We had it here at the farm, and one of my goats got out and tried to bust up the party." Ruby chuckled. "My boys ended up chasing that animal all over creation, and Ryder ripped his shirt on some barbed wire. We still laugh about that, and it's a good reminder of a real happy day."

"Ryder will treasure this quilt, Ruby. You've sewn some wonderful memories into it."

Ruby sighed. "They ain't all so wonderful. Like this one." She tapped a bit at the lighter end of the piece. "Can you tell what color this is?"

Elise leaned closer and squinted. "I'm not sure. Is it a very pale green?"

"Your guess is as good as mine. That cloth is so faded there just ain't no telling. Ryder was wearing that shirt when he came here, and it was a sorry-looking thing even then." She tsked her tongue. "All my kids came looking rough, but I do believe Ryder was the shabbiest of the lot. I figured this shirt would fall apart when I washed it, but it didn't. Kind of like Ryder himself, I reckon, held together by pure willpower. First thing I did after he got here was drive him down to the Walmart and buy him some new shirts." She shook her head. "I never seen any boy so grateful for a few cheap shirts. I kept this one for him in case he wanted it someday. You know, for sentimental reasons. But I reckon there wasn't anything in Ryder's past worth getting sentimental about, 'cause he never showed no interest. Fact is, he never talks much about his life before he came here."

"But you put this piece in his quilt anyway?"

"Well, sure." Ruby shot her a surprised glance. "Had to. It's part of his past, ain't it? That's the way life is, honey. Good times and bad times coming one after the other. You got to take 'em all together to get the beauty God intends us to have. It's the same way with people."

In spite of herself, Elise was curious. "How so?"

"Well, take Ryder, now. I don't know if you've noticed yet, but that boy's as generous as the day is long. Too generous sometimes. He's good at making money, and he's real smart with it mostly, but when it comes to his family, he spends it like water. I can't tell you how many times I've argued with him over some newfangled gadget he's just determined I have."

Elise remembered the dishwasher story—and a certain gigantic bouquet of flowers. "I think I understand."

Ruby gave her a thoughtful look. "I thought you might," the older woman murmured. "I used to get right frustrated with him. It's hard to make that boy see reason."

"I understand that, too," Elise assured her.

"But you know what? From the time these young'uns came into my care, I prayed over them that the Lord could bring good out of their troubles. And finally it dawned on me that this gift-giving business? That's God's work in Ryder.

That boy ain't said much about his past, but there was some things I didn't need to be told. He come up dirt poor. Didn't nobody look after that boy like they oughta have, and he'd gone without what he needed more than once. So, for him, bein' generous, buying folks gifts they don't really need, well, it's just his way of loving on them."

"Oh," Elise murmured. That made sense. She remembered her tart comment about money not being the solution to every problem and cringed. Ryder was right. She'd probably have a very different opinion if she'd ever gone without it.

Like he had.

"Not," Ruby added, beginning to fold up the half-completed quilt, "that he don't annoy the socks off me sometimes. We 'bout come to blows over a dishwasher once. Speaking of that, I reckon we'd better get on back to the kitchen. You don't mind pitching in with the dishes, do you, honey?"

"Not at all." Elise helped gather up the squares on her end of the bed, stacking them carefully.

A triumphant smile lit Ruby's face as she accepted the pile of squares, adding them to her own. "You're a good, sweet girl, as well as being pretty to look at. The Good Lord sure does know what He's doing."

"Excuse me?"

"Nothing, child. Just talking to myself. No,

never mind with the quilt. I'm not going to put it back in the wardrobe after all. I believe I'll spend some time later this evening working on it. I'm suddenly all afire to get the thing finished." She shook her head and chuckled. "You just never know when the Lord's going to move, do you?"

Ruby didn't seem to expect an answer, so Elise didn't offer one. As she followed the older woman out of the bedroom and back toward the kitchen, she puzzled for a moment over what Ruby might have meant. Then she shrugged and dismissed the confusing exchange from her mind.

She'd better focus on what she needed to say to Ryder, as soon as she could speak to him alone.

Apparently, she owed him an apology.

Chapter Eight

Her opportunity didn't arise until much later that evening. After she'd tucked the twins into bed, she came downstairs to find Ryder busily tapping on a laptop he'd set up on a desk in the living room.

"The boys are down for the night," she said.

He glanced up and smiled. "Thanks. I appreciate you staying later and getting them settled. It gave me a chance to catch up on some emails."

"Sure." She'd been stalling, waiting for this moment. Now that it was here, she wasn't sure how to start. She sat, perching on the edge of a chair. "It must be a challenge to balance your workload with the boys."

"It's not easy, but I'm managing. Thanks to you." He paused, looking uncertain. "And about the library thing. I want you to know—"

"Please." Elise violated Nanny Bev's rule by

interrupting him in midsentence. "You don't have to explain. I owe you an apology. The truth is, I was feeling a bit...worried...over something else entirely."

"Oh." Ryder seemed taken aback by her shift in attitude. "Well, no apology's necessary. It's got to be frustrating for you to be trying to teach me when I keep going rogue."

His eyes twinkled as if daring her to disagree. She smiled.

"Well, I have a few lessons to learn myself. You were quite right in what you said earlier—that money may seem less important to those of us who've never gone without it."

He looked uncomfortable. "I shouldn't have said that. I have exactly zero idea what it would be like to grow up with plenty of money, so I shouldn't be making any sweeping statements about it."

"No, you were right. Growing up with my father, money wasn't something I worried about. At least, not in the ordinary way. Money was more like a weapon—something my father used to get people to do what he wanted."

Ryder was watching her closely. She'd come to recognize the expression on his face, thoughtful and focused. He was reading her, trying his best to understand not only what she was saying, but what she truly meant. "I have a hunch that tactic didn't work so well with you."

"Not really. Although just lately, I've gotten a glimmer of what you're talking about—how a lack of money can be a crisis."

Ryder nodded slowly. "You said earlier that you were worried. That have something to do with money?" When she hesitated, he went on. "I'm not trying to pry, and your personal business is just that—personal. But unlike wrangling four-year-olds, money happens to be something I understand, and I'd be happy to listen and give you my thoughts. If you'd be interested."

Elise hesitated, but what he said made sense, and she'd been praying for some sort of guidance. Nanny Bev had been particularly fond of a fable about a foolish fellow perishing in a flood after refusing repeated rescue attempts.

"When the Lord extends a helping hand to you, grab hold," Nanny Bev had said. "Even if it comes from somebody unexpected."

"All right," she said. "There's a bit of difficulty with my old nanny's assisted living expenses. She's in a good care home, but the prices are going up."

Ryder listened carefully as she outlined the troubles, stopping her twice to ask for specific figures. When she'd finished speaking, he leaned back in his chair, frowning.

"You need more money," he said.

She laughed out loud. "Obviously."

He didn't smile. "I could pay you a little more, but—"

"Oh, no!" Surely he didn't think all this was some sort of elaborate attempt to get a raise. "I wasn't expecting you to do that."

"I was already thinking I should pay you more than we'd agreed on. It's only fair since you're teaching me in addition to looking after the children. The problem is, the amount I can currently afford isn't going to make up the difference."

"I wouldn't feel right about accepting more money anyway. I flatter myself that I'm worth the money when it comes to childcare. I've been professionally trained for that, and I'm reasonably good at it."

"You're a lot more than that."

"But I've no experience training adults, so it wouldn't be right for me to charge you for that."

"I think you're doing a great job at it. I'm just not the easiest person to teach. Anyway, the offer isn't based on your experience. It's based on the fact that I added to your duties. I am going to pay you more. That part's not open to debate. The problem is, I don't see that solving your problem, especially since you're only here for the summer."

"No." *Only here for the summer.* The reminder hit her squarely in her stomach. "That's true."

"Would the Shermans increase your salary enough, do you think?"

"Unlikely." She sighed. "I'm already being paid quite well, which was how I was able to help Nanny Bev in the first place."

Ryder looked thoughtful. "So what you really need is a side hustle."

"Side hustle?"

"That's right. Something you do on the side that brings extra money in. Have any other marketable skills?"

"I'm afraid not. I've only been trained to care for children. It's all I ever wanted to do."

"Don't sound so apologetic. There's no shame in that. Focus like that is great—and something a lot of people never find."

Funny how this man's praise made her grow warm and flustered. "However, it doesn't seem to lend itself to...what did you call it? A side hustle."

"Don't give up so fast. I'm thinking." He sat there silently for a minute, tapping a pencil on the notepad in front of him. "You'd need something portable. I mean, I'm assuming you're not going to be with the Shermans forever. Right?"

"Well, no. Children grow up, and nannies move on to new families. That's the way it works."

Ryder nodded. *Tap tap tap* went the pencil. "Any possibility that some of your nanny's other previous kids would step up and help pay for her care?"

"I don't see how it could be managed." She'd thought of that herself. "Nanny Bev was excellent at her job, and she stayed with her charges for quite some time. The man she nannied before me passed away in a car accident about ten years ago. Nanny Bev was devastated. I believe there was another family before that—two girls, I think, but from what I've heard of that family, I think charity doesn't list high on their roster of virtues."

"I see." *Tap tap tap.* "It's up to you, then. That's not a bad thing. Sometimes it's easier if you're the one making all the decisions. So, since you'll be moving around from location to location, there wouldn't be much point in building up a business locally."

"No." Elise's hopes dropped.

Ryder didn't miss the change in her expression. "Like I said, don't give up. Anyway, I've got an idea."

"You do?"

"How are you with computers?"

"Computers? That depends. I'm fairly adept at using them, but if you want me to build one..."

Ryder laughed. "No danger of that. Tell you what, let me sketch out a few ideas, maybe talk to my sister Torey, and I'll get back with you to-morrow."

"Oh, but I don't want you to take time away from your own work. I know you're staying up late as it is, trying to keep up."

"Not a problem. Don't worry about this any-more, Elise, okay? Leave it with me, at least for tonight."

She hesitated. She shouldn't let him take on her burdens. But he seemed awfully willing to help, and she really didn't want Nanny Bev to have to move.

"All right. And Ryder? Thank you."

He smiled. "You're very welcome."

That was all he said. The whole exchange had been nothing but kind and professional. So there was no reason for her heart to tingle warmly as she walked the short path to her little cottage, no reason for Ryder's smile to linger in her mind until she drifted off to sleep.

But it did, just the same.

The next afternoon, Ryder paced the living room as Torey's fingers flew over the computer keyboard.

"Can you hurry this up?" he asked, throwing an uncertain look through the window. No sign of Elise and the boys yet. "They'll be back any minute."

"Stop pestering." Torey didn't glance up from the screen, her brow puckered as she kept tapping keys. "I'm just cobbling this website together so you'll have something to show her, but even so, it takes a minute. You don't want it to look junky."

"No, I guess not." He peered over his foster sister's shoulder only to have her make a shooing gesture.

"Don't breathe down my neck. I'm almost done." Torey bit her lip and leaned forward, scrutinizing the screen.

"Good." Ryder's heartbeat sped up as a familiar car turned into the drive. "Because they're here."

"Go stall her for five minutes, then bring her in and I'll show her what I've got," Torey instructed him.

"Okay."

"But don't expect too much, not for two hours' work. I'm good, but I'm not that good."

"Yeah." Ryder tugged Torey's dark ponytail on his way to the door. "You *are* that good."

Torey yelped and swatted at him before refocusing her attention on the computer screen. "Five minutes," she reminded him.

Elise was helping Benji out of the back seat. Tucker stood beside the car, waiting on his brother. He was obviously impatient—he was bouncing up and down on the heels of his sneakers. But he was staying put, and he wasn't complaining.

Ryder smiled. He'd have to ask her how she'd managed that. Elise truly was amazing.

"Now," she said, tugging Benji's shirt into place and giving the twins a narrow-eyed look-over. "You have—" she paused to glance at her watch "—half an hour before lunchtime. You did quite a good job helping at the library, so you may skip tidying up your room and go play in your fort until then."

The two boys cheered and ran off toward the backyard, zooming by Ryder like twin tornadoes.

"Hi, Uncle Ryder!" they shouted as they passed.

He smiled and looked up to find Elise smiling back.

"I take it the library work session went well."

"We had a few bumps at the beginning," she admitted. "But they did quite well, all in all. The trick is to explain quite clearly what's expected, and to set a time limit. They knew they had to work for an hour with a ten-minute break in the middle." She took a small plastic timer out of her pocket. "Children work better when they know there's a time limit. They weren't terribly happy about pulling weeds, but in the end, I think they quite enjoyed themselves. Mr. Aldridge is a very nice man. A bit curmudgeonly, but not so bad with children once he warms up a bit."

"Good. I'm sorry I couldn't go with you, but Torey was free this morning, so I figured we'd get to work on your problem."

"Oh!" She was trying to disguise the hope she felt—he could see that. He used to do that, too, back when hoping had been a painful pastime. "And have you come up with anything that might work?"

"We think so." He glanced at his watch. Five minutes on the nose. "Come tell us what you think."

When they walked into the living room, Torey was still typing furiously. "Just. In. Time," she said, punctuating each word with a tap on the keys. "All done. For now," she amended, shooting an apologetic look at Elise. "Don't judge me by this. Like I told Ryder, this is a rough job. I can make it look a lot better when I have more time."

"Make what look better?"

Torey shot Ryder a questioning look, and he nodded. *Go ahead.*

She scooted away, revealing the screen. "Ta-da! Ask a Nanny!"

Elise's picture smiled from the computer screen. Ryder scanned the website with interest.

As usual, Torey had downplayed her skills. He might not be able to design a webpage, but he knew one that ticked off all the marketing checkboxes. This one looked perfect.

Elise walked toward the computer screen, looking bewildered.

"Ask a Nanny?"

"Ryder's idea. He says people everywhere you go ask you for tips, and he thought maybe a site like this could be a moneymaker for you."

Elise dropped into the chair beside Torey's, her eyes fixed on the computer screen. "This can make money? How?"

Torey shot Ryder a questioning look and waited until he nodded before answering. "People will pay to subscribe to your site. You'll offer some tantalizing appetizers for free, but to get to the real meat, people will pay. Plus, Ryder's used his ninja salesman skills to pull in some great companies who are willing to set you up as an affiliate marketer."

"Companies?" Elise frowned. "What kind of companies?"

"Nothing sketchy. Companies that make educational games, quality children's clothing, things like that," Ryder hastened to assure her. "They're all on that list there. You can review them, and if there are any you're unsure of, we can scratch them off."

"They're all reputable—and they represent serious money, no small feat for a beginning blogger, let me tell you. Ryder's also volunteered to take over your launch," Torey said.

"He has?" Elise darted an uncertain look up at Ryder. "That's—very kind. But you don't have to—"

"Take him up on it," Torey cut in decisively. "My brother's a pain sometimes, but he knows his business. He's giving you something for free that my clients pay thousands of dollars for." Torey grinned. "For that matter, so am I." When Elise's brow puckered, Torey went on. "This family helps each other. It's what we do. Now, let me show you how this thing works."

"That's so kind of you, but the twins are in the backyard and—"

"I've got them," Ryder said. "You go ahead and let Torey explain everything."

"It shouldn't take too long," Torey said. "Unless— How much do you know about computers, Elise?"

"Not that much."

"Okay. We'll start at the beginning."

Ryder walked to the backyard as Torey began her tutorial. The boys were happily playing in their beloved fort, their shouts blessedly muffled by the stout wood. He dropped down on the steps, pleasantly shaded by the large oaks.

The boys seemed happy, so he'd let them play in peace. That elaborate swing set, Ryder reflected for the dozenth time, had truly been an answer to prayer.

And, of course, so had Elise.

He hoped she liked the website idea. He hadn't been able to read anything on her face just now except for surprise. He'd pitched plenty of ideas like this—many of them in high-stakes situations. Sometimes his job had depended on how well his client liked the proposal he'd come up with.

Even so, he couldn't remember ever being more nervous than he felt right now.

It seemed an eternity before the door opened behind him.

"So, Elise? What do you think?" He turned around, but instead of Elise, Torey studied him, a humorous glint in her eyes.

"Sorry to disappoint," she said, quirking one eyebrow upward. "Elise is doing a dry run in there, trying to make a post. The site isn't live yet, so it doesn't matter if she messes it up. I'll get everything up and running as soon as she says the word."

"What do you think? Does she like the idea?"

"Hard to say." Torey leaned against the doorframe, her arms crossed in front of her chest. "This whole thing seems to have knocked her for a loop. Maybe you should have cleared this idea with her beforehand. You'll find out what she thinks in a minute, though, because she wants to talk to you."

Ryder frowned. He sure hoped this wasn't going to be a repeat of the whole flowers incident. "Is she upset?"

"How should I know?" Torey dropped down on the step beside him. "I don't study her like you do. Oh, don't deny it. You zero in on her like she's the only person in the world. Speaking of that." She tilted her head, looking at him speculatively. "I talked to Ruby."

"And?"

"And she was awfully happy about you bringing your Elise out there for supper. That's the way she put it. *Ryder's Elise.* Ruby thinks the world of her. And she's bumped your memory quilt up on her priority list. You know what that means. She believes the two of you are headed down the church aisle."

"Shhh!" Ryder threw an uneasy glance at the door behind them. No sign of Elise, thankfully. "Ruby's being ridiculous, and you know it as well as I do. Please don't bring that up, especially not when Elise is around."

"Oh, yeah." Understanding glinted in Torey's eyes. "Maggie mentioned something about her being none too happy about taking a job with a single father."

"Exactly, and I've made a couple of goofs that haven't helped. I don't need her finding out about Ruby's silly matchmaking."

"Yeah." Torey's lips twitched. "I heard about those flowers. Makes me wonder exactly how silly Ruby's being. Her track record's pretty good, you know. She's got two of us matched up already. And I haven't seen you go this far out of your way for a girl not related to you since back in high school."

Ryder groaned and rubbed his forehead. "I miss living in a city where nobody knows your business."

Torey gave him a sisterly slap on the arm. "Too bad. We like having you around. But if you're trying to convince Elise you're not interested, you might want to scale back some on the gifts and favors. Speaking of that, you'd better go inside and talk with her. I'll stay out here and watch the twins."

Ryder blinked. "You're volunteering to watch the boys?"

His sister shrugged. "For a few minutes, sure. They're a lot easier to handle now. Another reason for you to stay on Elise's good side. Now stop stalling and go talk to her. But don't take too long or I'll sell your two monkeys to the circus." This last remark was directed toward two freckled faces peering out of the fort.

It was answered by monkey-like hoots and screeches. As Ryder went into the house, Torey was hooting good-naturedly back, and he was shaking his head in grateful disbelief.

Torey had gone carefully quiet every time the twins were mentioned since the day she'd unwisely left her prized laptop unattended in Ruby's living room. By the time she'd returned, the boys had pried nearly all the keys off and were throwing them into the air like confetti.

Tuck and Benji hadn't exactly been in her good graces since then. Until now.

Ryder walked toward the living room, his brain setting up an impromptu presentation to sell Elise on the whole Ask a Nanny idea. It was a good strategy, and it would make money. His marketing instincts told him that, and he'd learned to trust them.

Getting Elise to trust them—or him—might be a problem, though.

She was still where he'd left her, sitting at the desk, leaning forward and peering intently at the computer. As he watched, she pecked at a few keys, then frowned and leaned back in her chair, studying the screen.

He cleared his throat, and she jumped.

"How's it going?" he asked.

That little pucker was running across her brow again. "It's rather a lot to figure out, but I think I'm getting the hang of it. Your sister acted as if this was all very simple, so I must be even worse with computers than I thought."

"Torey thinks everything related to computers

is simple. All that stuff's like breathing to her, and she can never understand why other people don't catch on as fast as she does. But you'll get the mechanics of it, I'm sure, and she'll help you with any questions that come up. She's already promised. The question is…" He dropped into an armchair and steadied his nerves with a deep breath. "What do you think about the concept?"

She looked at him. "It terrifies me." As his heart fell, she shook her head. "I mean, it's brilliant. And I'm almost afraid to believe what your sister said about the kind of money it could generate." Elise's eyes dropped to the printed spreadsheet Torey had brought along. "It would solve all my financial problems in one go. I can't…quite believe this is possible. Or that I could actually make a success of something like this."

"You could."

A smile flickered around her mouth. "You sound so certain."

"That's because I am. I don't know much about nannying, maybe. But I do know a viable business idea when I see one, and I do understand what people are willing to pay money for. This has tons of potential, Elise. You can just look at all the high-dollar companies we've got lined up—that tells you this is a gem of an idea."

The pucker deepened slightly. "Torey said you pulled in favors to get those."

"I pulled in favors to get to talk to the company reps about linking with your blog," he corrected her. "But that's as far as it went. Trust me, if they didn't see a moneymaking opportunity here, they'd never have signed on."

"Still, I'd never have been able to do this without your help." She met his eyes frankly. "And honestly? That makes me a little uncomfortable. I don't entirely understand why you'd go to such trouble to help me."

Ryder understood what Elise was saying. She figured there must be some strings attached to this offer, some hidden price that she was going to be expected to pay. If he couldn't convince her otherwise, this idea was going to be dead in the water.

The good news was, he'd prepared for this question.

"There are actually three reasons, if you'd like to hear them."

She looked surprised, but she nodded. "Please."

"First, I want to help you because I can. I understand what's marketable, and I have the professional connections to make this happen. This is what I'm good at, so when I see the opportunity to use my skills to help somebody, I do it." He smiled. "It's another thing Ruby drilled into all us kids. Whatever God's gifted you to do, do it. If you see a need you can fill for someone, fill it. The way Ruby sees it, that's all part of being a practicing Christian."

Elise tapped her pencil thoughtfully against her lips. "I can understand that."

So far, so good. "Secondly, I owe you a favor. The twins' behavior has really improved since you came on board."

"I would hope so. But you don't owe me anything for that, except my salary. It's my job."

"True, but I think there should be some extra compensation when a person does a job spectacularly—and you definitely have. When Tuck and Benji came to live with me, my life unraveled like a cheap sweater. I had no idea how to deal with their issues. I realize we still have a way to go, but now, thanks to you, the future's not looking so grim anymore."

Elise pressed her lips together, keeping them in a very professional straight line. She was trying not to react to his praise, but she wasn't fooling him. Smile or not, he could see the warmth in her eyes. "I'm happy you're pleased," she said quietly. "What's the third reason?"

"Nanny Bev."

She lifted an eyebrow. "Pardon?"

"She's my third reason. I'd like to help her, if I can."

"Well." A flicker of skepticism. "That's quite kind, considering you've never even met her."

"I don't have to meet her to know her. Let me guess. She's about fifty pounds of personality in a five-pound sack, right? She cuts you no slack and loves you without question. She was there for you when nobody else was, and she pulled you up out of the dark into a life you never even knew existed. And the funny thing is, she thinks she's nothing special. But the truth is, she's the most special person you've ever met." He waited.

"Oh." Elise's eyes were sparkling suspiciously. "You do know her," she whispered.

"Maybe not her specifically, but I know people like her. Or one person in particular. Your Nanny Bev sounds a lot like our Ruby, and I've got a soft spot for women like that. The world doesn't notice the huge difference they make, but the kids they take care of sure do. They roll up their sleeves and change the world, one child at a time." He smiled. "Speaking from experience here."

"You're absolutely right." This time Elise surrendered to her smile, allowing it to bloom. Ryder's breath caught in his chest—and his ability to think clearly flew out the window.

Dimly, in the last functioning corner of his brain, he realized it might be a good thing Elise was sparing with her smiles. They lit up her face, transforming her from pretty to—

Something more.

He was good with words. He always had been. But he couldn't think of the right word to describe Elise's face when she was smiling like that.

"So." He cleared his throat twice before he managed to go on. "If I can do something to help you make Nanny Bev's retirement more comfortable, I'd like to pitch in."

"You know, I believe you would." Elise spoke softly, wonderingly. "It's terribly kind of you. Ruby did mention how generous you tend to be." Her hazel eyes twinkled. "And that it didn't always go over so well. The dishwasher incident came up."

He winced. Ruby's reaction to the dishwasher had become a family joke, and he'd probably be teased about it for the rest of his life. "Yeah. Apparently, I'm not so good at figuring out what gifts women like." He gestured at the computer. "But this kind of stuff? This I am good at. Let me help you turn Ask a Nanny into an extra source of income. As a friend," he added quickly. "That's what friends do. We have a professional arrangement here, I know, but we're also friends. Aren't we?"

Elise blinked and looked away as she thought that question over. She was cautious—too cautious. Somebody in her past—somebody important—had done some serious damage to her ability to trust.

He'd dealt with that before. In his profession, he encountered plenty of people who'd been burned by salesmen and who weren't in any big hurry to trust another one, no matter how firm a handshake or how good a deal he offered them. It annoyed him, cleaning up messes dishonest people left behind, but he accepted it as part of the job.

Of course, he'd encountered it personally, too. All of his foster brothers and sisters had issues with trust, although they showed up differently. Ruby had always cautioned them to be gentle with each other's quirks, likening it to a physical injury.

If somebody's got a bad bruise, it don't matter if you didn't cause it. Don't matter if you don't understand it. You still got to be careful of that sore spot or you'll hurt 'em.

"You can trust me, Elise."

She looked back at him now, her eyes studying his face for a few careful seconds.

Finally, she swallowed hard—and nodded. "All right. Thank you, Ryder. For your help with this and for your friendship. I accept both."

He almost laughed—first because her answer was so oddly formal, and secondly out of sheer relief. Because stiff as it was, this wasn't a knee-jerk, polite answer. She meant it.

"Good!" On impulse, he got up, walked over

and held out his hand. "Let's shake on it." She hesitated a second before rising from her chair and accepting it.

He'd meant the handshake as a joke, but when his fingers closed over hers, there wasn't anything funny about the jolt that hit him.

He froze, standing there holding her hand, his eyes fastened on hers. She looked at him, her eyes wide and—for a moment there, at least—her expression sweetly unguarded.

He couldn't move. He just stood there staring at her, goofy as some schoolkid who'd bumped into his high school crush in the lunchroom line.

Maybe Elise was just as thrown as he was, because for a second or two she just stared back at him. Then her cheeks went bright pink. She pulled her hand free and stepped away. "Again," she said quietly, "thank you. I promise not to allow this new project to interfere with my job caring for the boys. Speaking of that, where are they?"

"In the backyard with Torey. Or being sold to the circus, depending on how things are going."

She didn't smile at the joke. "I'd better go take charge, then, don't you think?"

"Probably."

She nodded and walked briskly through the house toward the kitchen.

Ryder stood where she'd left him, waiting for

his nerves to quit jangling. Then he sucked in a breath and moved to shut his laptop.

His eye caught on the screen. Elise's face looked out at him, sweet and serious, her mouth primmed up in a very nanny-like line. He studied the image, his hand resting on top of the computer—until he realized he was smiling at the woman's picture like some sort of doofus.

He shut the laptop with a quick snap.

Friends, he reminded himself sternly. *Just friends*.

But for the first time in his life, he was afraid he'd made a deal he wasn't going to be able to keep.

Chapter Nine

A week later, Elise busied herself at the counter, keeping her eyes fixed on the grapes she was slicing in half. As old as the twins were, this precaution wasn't strictly necessary. But it gave her hands something to do and kept her from interfering as Ryder tried to convince the boys to sample the raw veggies served alongside their peanut butter and jelly sandwiches.

It wasn't going well so far, and every instinct Elise possessed was pressing her to step in—but, of course, she couldn't, not if Ryder was going to learn how to manage the boys effectively on his own.

"Broccoli is yucky," Tucker announced.

"Yeah!" Benji agreed. "We want tater chips."

"Potato chips are really good," Ryder agreed. *Find a point of agreement,* she'd told him. "I like 'em too. But these vegetables are just as crunchy, and if you dip them in the ranch dressing—"

"Uh-uh." Out of the corner of her eye, she saw Tucker push his plastic dinosaur plate away. Benji immediately followed suit—then thought better of it, pulled it back and snagged a triangle of sandwich. Then he pushed it away again and poked his lips out.

Elise bit down on the inside of her own lip and sliced another grape. *Steady,* she told herself. *Don't say anything. Let Ryder figure this out.*

"Well, you don't have to eat it if you're not hungry." Good. He was following another one of her instructions. *Never force food.* She mentally gave him a point. "Of course," Ryder went on, "it's kind of a shame. Kids who aren't hungry enough to eat their broccoli don't have enough room in their stomachs for dessert, either."

The twins exchanged a horrified glance.

"There's no room for broccoli," Tucker explained quickly. "But there's lotsa room for cookies."

Ryder chuckled. "Life doesn't work that way, kiddo."

"Them cookies," Benji whispered to his brother. "They're chocolate chip today. Them's our favorite."

Tucker shook his head and crossed his arms over his chest. "I ain't eating no broccoli."

"Your choice." Ryder reached for the plates. "But that means cookies are off the menu, too."

"I'll eat mine!" Benji grabbed his plate and slid it back into its place. When Tucker shot him an exasperated glance, his brother shrugged. "Chocolate chip," he repeated. He picked up a broccoli floret, doused it in the small cup of ranch dressing and crunched.

"It's not so bad," he assured his brother when he could speak again. "With all the white goop on there, you can't hardly taste the green stuff."

Elise fought a smile as she scooped the halved grapes into a plastic container and fitted the top on. All ready for the twins' snack later this afternoon.

She turned to go to the refrigerator in time to see Ryder pick up a floret of broccoli and turn it around in his hand. "You know what these look like? Little trees. Don't they?"

"Kinda," Benji agreed. Tucker stayed stubbornly silent.

"They're like tiny trees," Ryder went on thoughtfully. "And Benji's like a gigantic dinosaur, chomping on them."

"Rawr!" Benji said. "Look at me, Tuck! I'm a dinosaur, and you ain't!" He chomped enthusiastically—and with his mouth wide open. Elise averted her eyes and stuck the container of grapes into the fridge.

"I can be a dinosaur, too!" Tuck grabbed for his plate, snatched up a piece of broccoli and shoved it into his mouth, forgetting about the dressing. "Rawr!" He crunched loudly.

"Uncle Ryder?" Benji asked. "Do dinosaurs like peanut butter and jelly sammiches?"

"Every dinosaur I have ever met loves them," his uncle assured him seriously. He glanced up, and Elise caught his eye. She smiled, and he winked.

And the bottom dropped right out of her stomach. She turned away quickly, pretending to search for something in the refrigerator, hoping the cool air would chill some of the silly color out of her cheeks.

This was getting ridiculous. She had to stop overreacting every time Ryder looked her way.

The twin dinosaurs made short work of their lunch and in ten minutes were running out to their beloved fort, cookies in hand. As soon as the door banged shut behind them, Ryder plopped down at the table and let out a loud, relieved sigh.

"That went better than I thought it was going to," he admitted.

"You did quite well." Elise made a point to speak in a calm, even voice.

"It was going south, but I managed to pull it out in the ninth inning. Thanks to all your pointers."

Elise reached for the boys' empty plates, careful to keep her eyes away from Ryder's. "I don't think I can take the credit for this win," she said. "You remembered my instructions very well—"

"For once," Ryder interrupted ruefully. "Although I did go off script, didn't I? Sorry about the whole dinosaur thing, by the way. It pretty much wrecked the table manners we've been working on, but it was the best I could come up with in a pinch."

"It worked," Elise admitted. "No wonder you do so well in sales. Any man who can sell a four-year-old on broccoli can sell anything to anyone."

He laughed then, and she made the mistake of looking at him. When their eyes met, she felt her stomach go wobbly. *Stop it,* she told herself desperately. *Before he notices you looking at him like he's some sort of mouthwatering dessert—and you're on a no-sugar diet.*

She needed to keep her mind on the job—and only the job. She began rinsing the plates. "I think," she said, "that the real reason the twins are responding better to you has more to do with your confidence. Children react positively to an assured adult. It makes them feel secure. Safe."

"Is that so?" Ryder got up from the table. He picked up the boys' empty cups with two fingers and brought them to the sink, looking thoughtful. "It makes sense. It's the same thing in sales. If you act insecure, you make the customer doubt your product."

"Right. Even babies sense when their mothers are tense or out of sorts," Elise explained. She wished he wasn't standing quite so close to her. Not that he was crowding her or anything. He'd left a respectful distance. But somehow, having him right here beside her, so near that she could smell the soap he'd used this morning—well. It wasn't helping her wobbly stomach any. "I can't tell you how many times I've reassured a nervous mother that her baby doesn't like me better than her—that it's all about confidence."

"Wow, that's a brilliant insight." Ryder reached for his phone. "We should do a video about that for Ask a Nanny."

Elise forgot her no-eye-contact rule and looked at him in horror. "Another video?" She shook her head. "I don't think so."

"It's a great topic, Elise. We'll title it something catchy, like 'Your Baby Doesn't Hate You.' It's just the kind of thing a young mother would google at about three in the morning."

Elise made an exasperated noise as she set the rinsed cups in the top rack of the dishwasher. "How would you know what young mothers look up on the internet?"

"I don't," Ryder admitted cheerfully. "But you do. You just said this is something moms worry about. Besides, even though I've never parented a newborn, I can make an educated guess. Let me tell you, after the twins came to live with me, my Google history got really interesting."

"I don't want to do any more videos right now." She didn't so much mind the videos. It was having Ryder looking at her through the lens of the camera that made her go all dithery. And that was getting worse. The last video had taken six attempts before they'd managed to get a usable one.

"We should build up a good library for your subscribers, Elise."

"What? All ten of them?" Elise gave a sad chuckle. "I don't think there's any rush. You had me make that video on managing tantrums for the—what did you call it?"

"Permafreebie."

"Right—the thing they get for free for subscribing. But people aren't signing up."

"Yet," Ryder corrected her firmly. "Okay, so Ask a Nanny hasn't taken off. It's only been a week. This is going to be a success, Elise. I feel it in my bones, as Ruby would say. I ran another ad for it today, but I've been kind of busy with the twins, and I haven't had a chance to see how it's doing. Why don't you go check? You've probably picked up a few more subscribers."

She doubted it. She'd watched the website like a hawk for the first few days, but the disappointment had become too distracting.

She started to brush aside his request, but

when she glanced up, he was looking down at her. There was a perfectly respectable space between them, but her insides did their rollercoaster impression anyway.

Maybe checking the computer wasn't such a bad idea. "I'll run to the cottage and look, if you'll keep an eye on the boys."

"Sure thing."

As Elise hurried across the yard, she gave herself another silent scolding. Enough, she told herself, was enough. Ryder Montgomery had done her a favor—or he'd attempted to. And yes, that had been rather...endearing.

But that day when he and Torey had sprung the website idea on her, when he'd taken her hand, there'd been...something. A dangerous sort of spark. She'd felt it right away, and she suspected he'd noticed. His eyes had darkened, and he'd taken an awful long time to let go of her hand.

Not that she'd particularly minded. Which, of course, was a big part of the problem.

She walked inside and pressed the button to wake up her computer. As she waited, her gaze strayed to the window. Ryder was sitting on the steps, dappled with the last of the afternoon sunlight. He was wearing khaki shorts and a faded blue T-shirt, and he looked—

Never mind how he looked.

Elise dragged her eyes back to the computer

screen and clicked on the envelope icon to bring up the Ask a Nanny email account.

Then she stared. Blinked, and stared again.

She went to the door. "Ryder? Could you come here, please?"

Her voice came out a little too high-pitched, and he frowned as he pushed up off the step and headed in her direction.

"Is there a problem?"

Mutely she pointed to the computer screen. He studied her for an instant longer before leaning over to look.

His eyes widened, and a grin spread over his face. When their eyes met, Elise felt her own lips tilting upward.

"There are over two hundred subscribers," she said. "And I keep getting emails notifying me that more people have signed up. I can't quite believe it, but—"

Before she could finish the sentence, Ryder reached out, lifted her up in his arms and spun her around.

Ask a Nanny was perking up and looking strong. His idea had worked.

Ryder had experienced plenty of triumphs in his professional life, but even his biggest sale hadn't felt better than this. It was such a relief. For all his reassurances to Elise—and he'd believed them because the statistics and his own gut instincts told him they were solid—he'd still been uneasy.

Sometimes, no matter how much of a sure thing an idea seemed, no matter how many charts and graphs backed it up, the concept just... flopped. That risk had never bothered him too much before. He figured that was just part of the package, and he'd enjoyed the challenge.

But this particular venture was different. Ask a Nanny's success or failure would deeply impact Elise, and that...mattered.

He smiled up into Elise's eyes as her hair tumbled around them, blocking out the rest of the world. She looked startled, the expression on her face frozen in place as he twirled her around the tiny living room. He was suddenly aware of the warmth of her waist under his hands, of how close her face was to his own.

Reality kicked in the door. *What am I doing?*

He set her down on the floor with an awkward thump.

"I'm so sorry," he said desperately. "That was way out of line. I shouldn't have—" He stumbled to a stop, trying to read her face to see how much damage his momentary loss of good sense had caused.

He couldn't tell. She still looked dazed.

"I'm really sorry," he repeated. "I got carried away."

Elise blinked. Then she flushed, straightening her clothes and smoothing her hair with quick, efficient movements. "That's quite all right," she murmured. "It's an exciting moment."

A second wave of relief rushed through Ryder, weakening his knees. She didn't seem offended. Her cheeks were bright with color, but she didn't look angry. For a second, he'd seen a different expression on her face, one he couldn't quite place. Mixed with the understandable surprise, there'd been something else, a sort of shy joy.

As if maybe she hadn't minded as much as he'd expected. As if maybe she hadn't minded at all.

"Ryder?" One of her eyebrows arched up.

Good grief. What was he doing, standing here staring at her like an adoring puppy? He seemed determined to ruin this moment by getting himself in trouble.

He cleared his throat. "You're right," he said. "It's very exciting when a project takes off. Usually when something like this happens, sales teams find a way to celebrate. Maybe we should, too."

He left the invitation hanging, only half-spoken.

She smiled. "That sounds like a great idea to me. It's been a while since I had a good reason to celebrate, but if all these emails mean I may be able to pay for Nanny Bev's extra expenses—"

"I think that's exactly what they mean."

"Then a celebration seems appropriate. What do you suggest?"

"Dinner maybe?" An idea occurred to him. "There's this restaurant in town people like. It's perched on the side of the mountain, looking down over Red Hawk River. It's the only place close by with tablecloths and candles, so it's a popular spot for special occasions. You know, like anniversaries or first dates or…" He trailed off.

Elise was looking up at him, her face sweetly serious, that little pucker in her brow as she listened closely to what he was saying.

He appreciated that, he realized. That way she had of listening fully, of giving her whole attention to the matter at hand. Come to think of it, he'd never seen her looking at her phone—not once—while she was with the twins or when the two of them were talking together. She always gave the person she was with, child or adult, her undivided attention.

It was a simple thing—so simple it had taken him this long to even notice it. But it was also very refreshing in a world full of distractions to feel…valued.

No wonder the twins responded so well to her.

He had a sudden image of what it might be like to sit across from Elise at a table at Red

Hawk Inn, watching a sunset brightening the clouds over the tumbling river, seeing the colors reflected in her eyes.

"That sounds lovely," she was saying. And he thought *yes, it sure does.*

But then she went on. "I don't think the twins would enjoy it very much, though. Do you?"

The twins. Of course, she'd assume that Tucker and Benji would be included in their celebration. And they should be.

He didn't know why he hadn't thought of that.

"No," he admitted. "Probably not."

"But I'm sure there are some more casual places around, aren't there? And you should definitely ask your sister to join us as well."

"Torey?"

"She was so generous to set up the website, and she's been so gracious about answering all my emails. I'd love to treat you all to a supper out, if you're willing."

She wanted his sister to come along, too. So much for his goofy ideas. "I'll give Torey a call and see when she's free. And yeah, there are a few mom-and-pop style places around that would probably be a better fit for the kids, but you're not buying us supper. This will be my treat."

"No. This is the least I can do—"

"I insist. After all, we're celebrating *you.* The

guest of honor doesn't buy her own meal. House rules."

"That hardly seems fair, since I'm already in your debt for all this help. I think—"

"'Scuse me."

They both turned around. Benji had cracked open the door and was peeking in at them. Tucker stood behind him. As they watched, he frowned and whispered something into his brother's ear.

Benji nodded. "Wait a minute," he told the adults, then pushed the door shut.

Ryder and Elise exchanged amused glances.

"What's going on?" Elise murmured.

"No idea." Three loud knocks sounded on the door. "But I have a feeling we're about to find out."

"Come in," Elise sang out sweetly.

The door cracked open.

"*Now* you say 'scuse me," Tucker instructed Benji in a loud whisper.

"'Scuse me," Benji repeated carefully. "Tuck and me—"

Tucker thumped his brother on the head. "You're messing it up. *Tuck and I.*"

"That part don't matter." Benji thumped his brother back.

"It does, too!"

Ryder started to object, but before he could speak, Elise reached out and gave his forearm a quick, warning squeeze.

He went silent, acutely aware of her fingers warmly encircling his wrist.

"I'm gonna do it," Tuck was saying.

"No, you ain't. We flipped a coin, and I won," Benji argued.

Tuck poked his lips out in a sullen pout. "Do it right, then."

"I'm tryin' but you keep stopping me." Benji turned back to the adults. "Okay," he said. "'Scuse me, Nanny Elise—"

"And Uncle Ryder," Tuck prompted. Benji shot him a dirty look, and Tuck took a prudent step out of thumping range.

"Tuck and I wanna know if we could have another cookie since we ate all that broccoli."

"All of it," Tucker added. "Every bite."

"And we've been doing a lotta running around and climbing up and down outta our fort, so we're using up lots of energy."

"You forgot the most important word!" Tucker shot his brother a dagger-like look.

Benji scowled at his twin, then turned back to the adults and gave a long-suffering sigh. "Please."

"You've asked very nicely," Elise said approvingly. "As for the cookie, hmm. I'm not sure. Uncle Ryder? What do you think?"

He looked at her. Her hazel eyes twinkled, and her hand was still covering his wrist. One corner of her mouth twitched upward, and she squeezed his arm lightly.

She was suggesting he say yes to the cookie.

"Yes," he said without taking his eyes off hers. He'd have said yes to pretty much anything just then. As the boys cheered, he leaned forward, until his lips were just a whisper away from her ear. "You're not buying me dinner. Not for a thousand websites. I already owe you more than I can ever repay."

When he pulled back, she smiled at him—a smile that went all the way up into her eyes. "All right," she said. "Why don't you call Torey and see when she's available for dinner? Meanwhile, I'll get the twins their cookies."

"That'll work," he said.

He watched as she ushered the boys across the yard. It was a happy picture. The summer sun found golden glints in her hair as his nephews scampered around her like delighted—but obedient—puppies. When she beckoned them closer, they came. And when she pointed to the mat and murmured something, they obediently scraped off their sneakers before bounding into the kitchen.

His mind flipped back to what life had been like before she'd come. He'd been at the end of his rope, and—more importantly—the twins had been angry and miserable.

Somehow Elise had changed all that. And she wanted to buy him dinner.

"Call Torey," he instructed his phone.

"Calling Torey," the mechanical voice responded obediently. He tucked the phone under his chin as he walked onto the porch of Elise's little cottage.

As he turned to shut the door, he glanced in at the tidy, bright space and breathed in one last scent of it. It smelled like her, he realized. Soothing.

Like a place you went to rest and count your blessings.

"Hi." Torey's recorded voice spoke into his ear. "Not able to take your call right now. You know the drill."

She must be busy or already talking to somebody. His family never blew each other off. They'd been ignored as children until Ruby had taken them in, and they'd made a pact never to ignore each other. She'd call him back the minute she saw his name on her missed calls.

"Hey, Tor." He pulled the door shut. "Not an emergency, but call me when you can."

The phone didn't make it back into his pocket before it rang.

He smiled as he lifted it to his ear again. "That was quick. Hope you didn't stop in the middle of something. Like I said, it's not an emergency."

"Glad to hear it."

The deep voice didn't belong to Torey. Ryder frowned. *Man*, his brain categorized quickly. Older, going by the timbre of the voice. And with a certain casual arrogance that—thanks to his years in sales—Ryder recognized instantly.

Money and power. Whoever this man was, he possessed plenty of both.

"I apologize," Ryder said. "I was expecting another call. Ryder Montgomery here. May I ask who's calling?"

"Andrew Cooper," the man replied. "I believe you know my daughter, Elise."

Chapter Ten

Elise's father.

Ryder halted in midstride, halfway across the yard.

He'd gathered that Elise and her father had a somewhat rocky relationship. It might not be the best idea to have this particular conversation in the kitchen with her and the twins. At least not until he found out what the man wanted.

"Hello, Mr. Cooper. Are you trying to get in touch with Elise?"

"Not at the moment." A chuckle rolled across the line, and something about it made Ryder's fingers tighten over the phone. "My daughter's not in the mood to talk to me at present. We've had a bit of a…misunderstanding. No, Ryder, you're the one I want to speak with."

Ryder lifted an eyebrow, noting the deliberate use of his first name. It was an old school ploy to establish dominance and authority. It was also a game two could play. "Oh? And what, exactly, is the reason for this conversation, Andrew?"

There was a short, pointed silence followed by a creak of leather and a rustling of papers. Yeah, definitely old school, Ryder decided. The sort of man who'd be impressed by Italian shoes, excellent steaks and a pricey country club membership.

"You're an interesting fellow, Ryder Montgomery. Your life reads like one of those motivational before-and-after stories. Foster care foundling to fast-rising sales executive. You had a hardscrabble beginning, including a couple of brushes with the law, but from what I see here—" another rustle of paper "—and from what I've heard from people who know you well, you've overcome that. Bob Terrance assures me you have excellent prospects. He predicts your new sales consultant business is going to be a colossal success."

Bob Terrance—his last supervisor before he'd launched out on his own. So Cooper had done some sort of background check. Ryder was liking this man less and less. No wonder Elise was on the outs with him.

"Glad to hear it," Ryder replied dryly.

"A real up-and-comer. That's what Bob said." Another oily chuckle rolled through the line. "And you and I both know Bob's never too free with his praise. He shared your last sales numbers with me."

"He did what?" The surprise slipped out. Bob Terrance shared sales stats with nobody outside the company.

"Relax. They were impressive. Bob and I are old friends, and he's always found it's in his best interest to be cooperative when I ask for favors. We had a very pleasant lunch yesterday, and you were the primary topic of conversation."

"Flattering. And confusing. Why, may I ask, am I so interesting to you, Andrew?"

"I understand my daughter's currently caring for your twin nephews." Another rustle. "Your late sister's children. My condolences on your loss. Tucker and Benjamin, I believe are their names?"

It wasn't really a question. Cooper was well-informed. "She is. And she's doing a spectacular job."

"Of course she is. These nannying jobs are well below her capabilities, and quite frankly, they're an embarrassment. My daughter's social standing is equal or above that of the people employing her. The idea of her scuttling their offspring to dance classes and music lessons is ridiculous. I'd intended to spend the summer convincing her of that, but you've spoiled my plans."

"Have I."

"Indeed. I'd extended an invitation to Elise to summer here with me. In fact, I'd gone to quite a good bit of trouble and expense to make the necessary arrangements. She's my only child, so naturally I'm concerned about her and would like to spend time with her. However, she refused in order to accept the position with you."

"I'm thankful she did."

"You'll excuse me for not sharing that sentiment," Andrew Cooper responded dryly. "Normally, I get very irritated with people who spoil my plans. However, in your case, I admit I'm intrigued."

"How so?"

"Let me be blunt, Ryder. You're not at all the sort of man my daughter usually likes. And yet, from what I've heard, she seems to be getting along with you quite well. By all accounts you seem quite taken with her, as well. Some flowers were mentioned, I believe."

Ryder frowned. "Whatever private investigator you hired did his job well."

"I only deal with the best."

That must be true. Any stranger poking around Cedar Ridge asking nosy questions would have stood out like a sore thumb. Somehow, this person had escaped detection—and turned up a lot of accurate details.

"I think this conversation has gone on long

enough. If you want to talk to your daughter, contact her directly."

"Now, now. I apologize for offending you, but bear in mind, at the time I had no idea who you were. You can understand a father's concern for his only daughter."

Ryder hesitated. Yeah, he could understand that. "Fine. That bought you five minutes to get to the point of this call, Mr. Cooper," he said, dropping the whole name arm-wrestling match. Let this guy feel like he had the upper hand. Ryder didn't care.

This man wasn't someone he wanted to be on a first-name basis with.

"Assertive. I appreciate that. I like you, Ryder. Or," the man amended with another chuckle, "I like the idea of you. Granted, you don't have the breeding I'd have chosen for my daughter, but at this point, I'm willing to overlook that."

"Chosen?"

"A poor choice of words. I should have said 'preferred.' As her father, I'm allowed to have preferences regarding a potential son-in-law, surely."

"I'm afraid you're mistaken. My relationship with your daughter is a professional one."

"Is it? You always send two-hundred-dollar bouquets to the women in your employ? And according to what I hear, your foster mother believes this relationship is a great deal more than a professional one."

Ruby. Ryder pressed his lips together tightly. "My foster mother is also mistaken."

"No need to deny it. As I said, I'm not objecting. You're in sales, so you understand. It's all in how you spin it. You're a self-made man, something most people in my circles respect. The ones who don't can be…influenced…to think differently, particularly once you attain a certain level of financial success. A level I can easily help you reach."

The implied offer dangled like a ripe plum on the end of a branch. "Thanks, but no thanks."

"Think carefully, Ryder." A hint of steel crept into the other man's voice. "A man with great capacity to help you can also hurt you, if he's properly motivated. The Shermans will only be in Europe for so long, and they plan to continue employing my daughter once they return. I'd rather they didn't, but I've already interfered as much as I can there without causing additional problems. That's where you come in. I would very much like to see Elise give up this nannying nonsense and take her rightful place in society—as the wife of a successful businessman, for instance."

This man had an incredible nerve and an incredible lack of respect for his daughter.

Nannying nonsense. Ryder recalled the amazing difference between how Tuck and Benji had behaved a few moments ago, and how they'd behaved when he'd first brought them home to Cedar Ridge. The way Elise helped the children in her care was not nonsense.

And neither was her reason for doing it.

"Do you know why your daughter took the job with me, Mr. Cooper? She's helping pay for her old nanny's living expenses in England. If you want to give her more leeway to spend her summers at leisure, maybe you should butt out of her personal life and put your money where your mouth is. This conversation is over. I'd suggest you not call me again."

He ended the call. He didn't bother to slip the phone back into his pocket. Torey would be calling any second. He'd been alerted several times during the conversation with Cooper that another caller was on the line, and he'd known it was his sister.

Torey was the family hedgehog—dangerously prickly on the outside, but cute and funny if you could ever get her to lower her defenses. And, like the rest of Ruby's bunch, she was ferociously loyal. She'd call, if she wasn't already on the way over, ready to fuss at him for not answering his phone.

How had Andrew Cooper described his life? A hardscrabble beginning and a lack of breeding? Maybe so. But he'd take his family life over Cooper's any day.

Just as he'd expected, the phone shrilled urgently.

"Hi, Tor."

"Well, it's about time." His sister's voice was sharp, but he heard the loving worry behind the tone.

"Sorry. I was on another call and couldn't get away. Anyhow, I've got some good news. Elise just checked on the website, and we have some serious celebrating to do. You in?"

There was a short hesitation. "I don't want to horn in on anything."

"You won't be."

His sister snorted. "Yeah, right."

Ryder shook his head. Looked like Ruby and Andrew Cooper weren't the only ones with certain ideas in their heads.

"Elise specifically asked me to invite you."

"Did she? That was nice of her." A new warmth tinged Torey's voice. The hedgehog uncurled a little. "Okay. Sure. I'm free tomorrow night."

"Not anymore, you're not."

After ending the call, he glanced toward the house. He had to tell Elise about her dad's call—and he didn't want to. This was really going to upset her, and he hated the thought of spoiling this happy day.

He especially hated the idea of disclosing Andrew Cooper's notions regarding Ryder and Elise's relationship. Having her dad's stamp of approval wouldn't likely be a mark in his favor, and for good reason. The idea worried—and infuriated—him, but there was nothing he could do about it.

Because, he told himself firmly, keeping the call a secret wasn't an option. On the other hand, there was no point ruining her happiness over Ask a Nanny's success. The bad news would keep for a day or two.

He'd tell her after their celebration dinner, he decided with a feeling of guilty relief. The very next morning.

Then he'd tell her everything.

The next evening, Elise was sitting not at a kid-friendly restaurant but at Ruby Sawyer's kitchen table, in a room crowded with Ryder's family. The last strains of "For She's a Jolly Good Nanny," sung off-key but with gusto, was followed by laughter. And then scattered clapping as Maggie Hamilton unfolded a large white bakery box, revealing a gigantic cake, festively decorated with icing ribbons and flowers.

"I'll carry that to the table," Maggie's husband, Neil, offered.

"No way. I spent all afternoon on this thing,

and nobody's carrying it but me." Biting her lip, Ryder's sister carefully transferred the cake to the table. Once it was safely in front of Elise, Maggie reached into her apron pocket, produced a lighter and lit a trio of slim tapers on top of the cake. They sizzled into sparklers, making the children squeal with delight.

Elise stared at the immense dessert and at the friendly, expectant faces around the table, completely at a loss.

How did you thank people for this? She had no idea.

Ryder had spent the whole drive here apologizing. Apparently his plan for a celebration dinner at a local restaurant had fallen apart the minute Torey had told the family about Ask a Nanny's success. They'd insisted on being included in the celebration. Before she knew what was happening, the dinner had been relocated to Ruby's home, and Ryder's foster brothers and sisters were all coming.

"It's what we do," Ryder had explained sheepishly. "We've got this all-for-one, one-for-all mentality going on. We stand by each other when there's trouble, but we make a point to celebrate together, too."

"Oh, of course. You and Torey set up the website, so they want to congratulate you." That made sense.

"Partly." He'd slanted a smile at her. "But don't get your hopes up. The focus tonight is definitely going to be on you. They all really appreciate what you've done for the twins, and as long as you're in Cedar Ridge, you're part of our family. At least, that's the way Maggie put it."

She'd agreed, of course. What else could she do?

The minute she'd arrived, she'd been swarmed with hugs and congratulations. It was wonderful, but also overwhelming. A whole family full of people so willing and apparently delighted to celebrate her success—she'd never experienced anything like it.

And now, this cake.

She blew out the sparkling candles with some difficulty, prompting a round of applause.

"I—don't know what to say," she managed past the lump in her throat.

Tucker tiptoed up beside her. "When Aunt Mags make you a goodie, you're s'posed to say thank you," he whispered helpfully.

The table erupted into affectionate chuckles, and Logan ruffled the boy's hair.

For some reason, that made the tears in her eyes spill. She dabbed at them and laughed at the same time. "You're exactly right, Tucker. Thank you so much, Maggie. And thanks to all of you for celebrating with me. It's so very kind."

Maggie enveloped her in a warm, vanilla-scented hug. "Don't be silly," she whispered. "Of course we're going to celebrate with you! And I hope you enjoy the cake, because later I'd like to ask your advice about a few behaviors we're struggling with at home."

"I heard that," Ryder said, poking his sister. "Trying to get freebies, are you, instead of subscribing to the website like everybody else?"

"Absolutely."

"Shameless," Ryder said. "That's what you are."

Maggie laughed and stuck out her tongue. "And exactly how much did you pay for this cake, *brother*?"

Ryder laughed back. "Point taken, but that was a favor for me, not Elise."

"Of course, Maggie, I'll be happy to offer any advice I can," Elise interjected belatedly, but the siblings didn't seem annoyed with each other. She watched as Maggie plopped fat slices of cake on plates and handed them around. She noticed Ryder scored an extra sugar rose accompanied by a sisterly elbow to the ribs.

This family was loud, and as subtle as a train whistle, and they adored each other. As a nanny, she'd had a front row seat to a variety of family dynamics, and she'd never seen anything quite like what she saw here. They jostled each other playfully, teased each other mercilessly, kept a watchful eye on each other's children and treated Ruby as if she were made of spun glass.

Elise took a bite of her cake—which was absolute perfection—and studied Ruby, who was sharing bites of her dessert with the toddler enthroned on her bony knees. Amazing what this woman had accomplished, Elise thought. Somehow in this tiny house, she'd taken a group of very mismatched people and formed them into a family.

"I'm so happy for you!"

Elise looked up to find Charlotte beaming at her. "Oh! Thank you so much."

"I'm not a bit surprised, though. I knew from the moment you took charge of the twins at the park that you were extraordinary." Charlotte leaned over and gave her a one-armed hug. "Thanks for letting us all celebrate with you." She leaned a bit closer and murmured, "This bunch can seem pretty overpowering at first, but don't worry. You're fitting into the family just fine."

Fitting into the family. That phrase lingered with her as the group chatted, laughed and congratulated her one by one. An hour later, when she didn't think it would be noticed, she slipped out of the crowded kitchen. Ryder intercepted her before she made it to the front door.

"Something wrong? Are we getting on your nerves?"

"Not at all. You're all being wonderful. I'm an only child," she reminded him with a laugh. "So I just need about five minutes to myself, and I'll be right back in for another piece of that cake."

"All right." Ryder stepped back. "But if it gets to be too much and you want to go home, just let me know."

She nodded and smiled, then walked outside.

Compared to the chaotic kitchen, the front porch of the farmhouse was cool and blessedly quiet. Elise stood on the creaking floorboards, studying the spill of stars over the sky as the cool mountain breeze fanned her flushed cheeks. A murmur of muffled laughter swelled behind her, accompanied by a sweet high trill coming from the surrounding trees. Some sort of insect maybe—or frogs? She didn't know, but whatever it was, it sounded friendly.

The whole place felt friendly and welcoming, and she knew that had more to do with the people she'd left back in the kitchen than the farm itself. It was funny. She'd been around families who'd enjoyed every advantage wealth could offer, but she'd never envied any of them as much as she envied Ruby's kids right now.

"Elise, honey?" The screen door behind her cracked open, and Ruby peered through her glasses. "What're you doing out here all by your lonesome? You all right?"

"Oh, yes. Just soaking up this beautiful night."

"And a little peace and quiet. I don't blame you a bit for sneaking off." Ruby chuckled as she came out on the porch. "My bunch gets kinda rambunctious when they're all together."

"You have a beautiful family."

"Well, thank you. I made it myself." Ruby cackled at her own joke and gave Elise's arm a playful slap.

"And you did a great job."

"No, honey, I was just joshing. I can't take the credit. The Good Lord brought them kids to me, one after another." She stood beside Elise, looking over the mountains, her smile barely visible in the starlight. "Him and me are still working together, growing this family, even now. Step by step, He's bringing my children their special folks, the ones they're meant for. First Maggie found her Neil, and then Logan and Charlotte. And now..." Ruby tilted her head up toward Elise. "You're here, and I got a feeling in my bones that God's working on Ryder."

"Oh!" Elise wasn't sure what she was supposed to say to that. "I don't—we're not—"

Ruby flapped a hand at her. "Save your breath. You think I didn't hear all that from Maggie and Logan too? My kids go into relationships kicking and screaming, but once they settle down, they build real strong families. They know how, you see, 'cause they understand the broken places so good. Take Ryder, now. He's been let down so much by other people that he has a horrible fear of doing it to other folks. Like the way he was scared he wasn't going to be able to be a good daddy to the twins because he never had a father worth his salt himself."

"Yes." Elise's heart twinged. "He mentioned something about that."

"But in the end, that just made him more determined to do his best. 'Course, he's doing even better now since God brought you along. And I can't help but think the Good Lord's got something else up His sleeve where the two of you are concerned. I see how he looks at you, 'specially when you ain't looking at him." Ruby chuckled. "That's always how it starts. And unless I miss my guess, you're feeling some flutters of your own. Ain't you?"

Flutters? Once again Elise found herself at a loss for words.

She should talk about professionalism and things like that. But somehow, her mind flashed back to Ryder—how he looked when he laughed. How he'd spun her around when she'd told him the news about the website.

She couldn't say no to Ruby's question. Not honestly. So she didn't say anything at all.

Even in the dim light, Elise could see the speculative glint in Ruby's eye.

"Ah." Ruby sighed. "God does like to test my patience. Bringing two skittish folks together can be a real long game. So, what's the problem? You got a family history that's turned you off relationships? Or an old boyfriend?"

"Both," Elise heard herself confessing. She didn't know why. She'd never talked about this before, except with one person. Maybe that was the reason. This plainspoken little woman reminded her a great deal of Nanny Bev.

"That so? What happened?"

She laughed self-consciously. "Let's just say my father's not as successful a matchmaker as you are."

"Oh, I'm sorry, honey. Yes, matchmaking can go wrong, if you leave God out of it. That's my secret. I just pray for all I'm worth, and I wait to see who the Lord brings along. When you take the reins in your own hands, it don't usually end well."

"My situation certainly didn't. It's why I was reluctant to take this job in the first place. I accepted a job with a single father once before, and it turned out to be a setup. My father had arranged the whole thing, even promising the guy a promotion if he could get me to marry him and stop working as a nanny."

"Oh, my." Ruby clucked her tongue. "And my kids think I'm a nuisance."

"They don't know what a nuisance is. My father's in a class by himself. At least you're honest with your kids about what you're doing. My dad pretended not to know anything about the man, to be suspicious of him, and the whole time they were having phone conversations about me behind my back." That memory still made Elise cringe.

"Then you found out."

"Only thanks to the man's ex-wife. It was awful at the time, but she did me a favor. Trust me, I'd never want to end up with someone who'd keep secrets like that—or any man my father approved of."

"Can't say as I blame you for that." Ruby studied her thoughtfully. "And what would that daddy of yours think about my boy in there?"

That question had been lurking in the back of Elise's mind for a while. She wasn't sure. Her father wasn't always predictable. But Ryder was different from the other men her father had pushed at her.

He was kind, for one thing. And willing to put himself out for others, like taking in his orphaned nephews. She certainly couldn't imagine her dad doing anything like that. And then there was Ryder's background. She could imagine what Andrew Cooper would have to say about a man who'd spent his childhood in the foster care system.

Ruby smiled. "Judging by the look on your face, Ryder wouldn't make the grade. So I reckon he's still in the running."

"Ruby—" Elise began.

"Never mind, honey. No point talking about it yet, anyway. I got a quilt to finish first." Ruby breathed deeply of the mountain air. "It's a real nice night, isn't it? You stay out here as long as you want, but I'd better get myself back inside. If I don't, my kids will flock out here looking for me, sure as the world."

"Ruby?" Elise called after her. The older woman paused, her hand on the screen door. "Thank you. For having me over and making me feel like family."

Ruby chuckled. "Oh, honey. You are family. You just don't know it yet." With that, she disappeared into the house.

Elise watched her go, listening to the happy murmur of voices inside. Of course, Ruby was just being polite. And maybe meddling a bit, but it was impossible to hold that against her.

For a moment, Elise wondered what it would be like to be a part of Ruby's flock. To be accepted and appreciated for who she was. To be celebrated and supported.

To be loved.

Her mind flitted to Ryder and the twins, and for just a second, she let her imagination step through a door she'd been keeping strictly off-limits. A picture rose up in her mind's eye of her and Ryder and the boys…together. A family.

Her heart didn't flutter—Ruby was wrong about that—it skipped and then thumped so hard she pressed her hand against her chest.

"Elise?"

She gasped and turned around to see Ryder standing in the doorway.

"Sorry if I scared you—and sorry to bother you. But you left your phone on the table and it's been going off about every two minutes. I thought maybe it was something important." He walked over and handed it to her.

She accepted it absently, looking up at him, her mind reluctant to leave its daydreams behind. He was gazing over the starlit mountain view. When he saw her watching him, he laughed.

"No place like home," he said. "This old house has always been my home base, and I love it. But now, with the twins, I need to put down some roots of my own. I'm thinking about putting in an offer on the Hickory Street house."

Elise blinked. "You're buying the house?"

"The boys really love that fort, and it's in a good neighborhood. What do you think?"

She tried to marshal her thoughts. "It might be a wise move. Stability is so important for children, and—"

"No," Ryder said softly. "I'm not asking for your professional opinion. I meant, what do you think of the house? Do you like it?"

Her heart pounded harder. Why was he asking her that question? "I do," she said. "It's…a beautiful house. It has a homey feel to it."

"That's what I thought too."

He seemed about to say something else, but before he could, the phone in her hand vibrated furiously. She glanced down and frowned.

"It's the Shermans." She hadn't heard from them since she'd hugged the girls goodbye at the airport. "I'm sorry. I'd better take this. There might be some sort of problem—"

"Of course. I'll be inside." Ryder gave her a last smile and started for the door.

Elise accepted the call. "Hi, Mr. Sherman! Is everything all ri—" She broke off, listening to the torrent of words. "What? No, of course not. Let me explain. It's just—"

It was too late. The call disconnected with a beep, leaving Elise staring dumbfounded at the screen.

"Elise?" Ryder had halted at the door, looking concerned. "What's wrong?"

"I—" She couldn't finish the sentence.

He crossed the porch fast. He tilted up her chin, his eyes searching hers. "What is it?"

She swallowed. "I just got fired."

Chapter Eleven

"What?"

"Jon Sherman just fired me," Elise repeated. Her voice shook, and her eyes were wide with shock. "He was...he was furious...yelling."

"At you?" When she nodded, Ryder felt his temper slipping. He didn't like the look on Elise's face. And he'd sure like to have a conversation with the man who'd put it there. "That doesn't make sense. Why?"

"Someone told him about the website, and he looked it up. He read some of the posts and watched a few of the videos where I explain how to deal with misbehaving children. He thinks I'm talking about his daughters."

Ryder frowned. "Why? There's a disclaimer on it that clearly states the examples aren't based on specific children you've worked with. No names were ever mentioned, and there aren't any identifying details."

"Of course not! I was very careful about that. And honestly, the Sherman girls weren't even that hard to manage. They were a bit difficult to start with, but they settled down fairly quickly. I've no idea why he's so insulted, but he was certainly in no mood to listen to my explanation."

It wasn't chilly on the porch, but she kept rubbing her arms. Impulsively, Ryder reached out and took her hands. They were cold, and they trembled in his.

"Don't worry about it," he told her, his voice gruff with sympathy. "It's upsetting, I know, but—"

"It's very upsetting." Elise's voice broke. "I'm quite fond of Payton and Bella Sherman. I hate to think they might believe I would betray their family's confidence, but I'm sure that's what their parents will tell them."

"That doesn't make it true."

"Then there's Nanny Bev," she went on. "I was just getting hopeful that I could swing the price increase, but now, without a permanent nannying job, there's no way I can manage. She'll have to move, and that's so hard at her age."

"Nanny Bev's going to stay right where she is. Don't worry. We'll find a solution."

"That's very kind, but this isn't your problem. Oh!" She looked startled, as if something had just occurred to her. "Please don't feel in any way that this is your fault, because of course it isn't. You had no way of knowing the website would upset the Shermans."

"Even so, I'm just as responsible for this mix-up as you are."

"No." Elise shook her head miserably. "I should have thought it through. You don't have the experience with parents that I have. People are extremely protective of their children. And of course, a nanny knows so much about any family she works with. It's natural they'd worry about gossip. I should've expected something like this and been prepared for it."

"I don't see what you could have done differently. This Sherman guy is being hypersensitive, and it makes me wonder what he's hiding. Ruby has an old saying—'It's the dog that's been bit that hollers the loudest.' Sherman's doing a lot of yelping for an innocent dog, if you ask me."

Elise didn't smile, and his heart tightened.

"Hey." He used the tip of his finger to tilt Elise's chin upward until she was looking into his eyes. "It'll be all right. You're not alone, Elise. We'll figure this out."

He was used to people viewing his promises with suspicion because salesmen were always suspect. So when a deal came down to the wire, he'd learned the importance of eye contact and sincerity. Now he did everything he could to put what was in his heart on his face, so she'd understand he meant exactly what he was saying.

He must have managed it, because he saw her expression shift, just a little. A cautious relief and hope dawned in her eyes. She'd decided to trust him, and the magnitude of that flooded his heart with relief and joy…and something else, stronger and sweeter and more determined than anything he'd ever felt before.

It was that—and maybe the way the starlight reflected in her eyes—that undid him. He closed the gap between them and covered her lips with his.

The kiss was short and sweet, but he felt the jolt of it all the way to his knees—which promptly turned to jelly. Then, about two blissful ticks too late, his common sense kicked in, and he drew back.

She was staring at him, her expression stunned. He didn't blame her.

He was feeling pretty stunned himself.

"I…uh…" He'd talked his way out of more than one tight spot in his time, but right now he couldn't think of a single word to say. He hadn't felt so flabbergasted by a kiss since his very first one.

And oddly, kissing Elise reminded him of that moment as no other kiss ever had.

She wouldn't have to leave now, he realized suddenly. Without the job with the Shermans waiting for her, she was free to stay in Cedar Ridge.

If she wanted to.

"Elise—" he started. That was as far as he got.

"What's going on out here?" Logan cracked open the door and stuck his head out. "Everything all right?"

Ryder swallowed, and he saw a flash of panic in Elise's eyes. She didn't want anybody to know about that kiss, he realized. Which was fine. He didn't either.

Well, part of him wanted to shout it from the rooftops. But the part of him that still had a functioning brain cell or two knew that wouldn't be the best idea. They had some ground to cover first.

The trouble was, he wouldn't lie to Logan. None of them ever did. Logan had a thing about lies. He'd grown up with too many, and he hated them.

Besides, he could sniff them out a mile away, so the only thing to tell him was the truth.

"Elise just got some bad news."

"Oh?" Logan stepped onto the porch. "Anything I can help with?"

"I'm afraid not," Elise said.

"Maybe," Ryder said at the same time. "She just got fired from her regular nannying job because of the website."

"What?" Torey's voice echoed from inside the

living room. She had hearing like a fruit bat. "Why?"

"What's going on?" Charlotte's voice was more muffled.

"Elise lost her permanent nannying job because of the website!" Torey called back. This announcement was followed by sharp exclamations of dismay from the kitchen.

The house erupted, the family pouring out onto the porch. They surrounded Elise with sympathetic indignation, demanding explanations. They led her back into the house, all talking at once. Elise cast one quick look at Ryder, but she didn't protest.

He stayed where he was. His mind was still too mixed up from that kiss to think clearly, and he didn't dare go inside until he'd gotten himself straightened out.

As the last of them crowded through the doorway, Ruby hung back. She studied Ryder, propping open the screen door.

"You coming, son?"

"In a minute." He needed a second to think about what had just happened and to figure out how to go forward.

He could feel his foster mom's sharp eyes on him. "Don't take too long, now. That girl needs you."

The light was too dim to see Ruby's expression, but he didn't have to. Somehow, she knew. He could hear the smile in her voice.

The next morning, phone in her hand, Elise returned to the kitchen, where Ryder was supervising the boys' breakfast. She halted in the doorway, looking at the scene in front of her.

The three of them were seated around the breakfast table. Her eyes were drawn to Ryder, and a now-familiar tickle started deep in her stomach.

That had been happening a lot lately—and since that unexpected kiss yesterday evening, it had ramped up considerably. She could barely look at Ryder now without feeling a wash of warmth and…affection.

That was the best word for it, she told herself cautiously. It certainly wasn't—it couldn't be— anything more than that.

They hadn't talked about the kiss yet, but she knew that conversation was coming. It hung over them like a rain cloud. So far there hadn't been much of a chance. The twins had kept them busy, and once they'd gone to bed, she'd pleaded exhaustion and slipped away to her cottage.

She'd seen the way Ryder had looked at her then, but he hadn't argued. She had a feeling he wasn't sure how to approach this either.

At the moment, however, he had another issue to deal with.

"I don't want scwambled eggs today. I want fried eggs," Tuck was complaining.

"I know, bud. But we're having 'em scrambled this morning."

"They're yucky." Tucker poked out his lips and shoved his plate away.

Elise considered the child's sulky face with concern. Tucker hadn't been that stubborn about food in a while. Likely the child was reacting to the tension he sensed between her and his uncle. Children often regressed when their caregivers were stressed out.

She watched Ryder thinking over the situation. He was getting better at this, she realized with a tiny smile. He didn't jump into arguments anymore. He thought them over and planned how to react. Maybe he didn't always react quite the way she would have, but he managed to pull off a success more often than not.

"That's because you're not eating them right." Ryder broke off a piece of the bacon on Tucker's plate and crumbled it into the scrambled eggs. Then, to Elise's horror, he reached for a tiny bottle of hot sauce and splashed a dollop onto the concoction. "See? That's how your other uncles and I eat scrambled eggs. Breakfast of champions, Tuck. Try a bite of that and see if you like it any better."

Hot sauce? For breakfast? Elise started to protest, then bit her tongue and waited.

Tuck didn't look too convinced, either, but curiosity got the best of him. He picked up a chunk of bacon-studded scrambled egg in his fingers. She winced at the breach of table manners and braced for an explosion. She had a feeling she'd be cleaning up a spewed mouthful of half-chewed eggs.

Instead, Tucker's expression shifted from suspicion to surprise.

"Good," the child mumbled with his mouth full.

Ryder smiled, and Elise's smitten heart dropped into her stomach with a thump. "Glad you like it. But next time, use your fork, okay?"

"Fix mine like that, too, Uncle Ryder!" Benji pushed his plate forward.

Boys. Elise shook her head ruefully. She hadn't seen that coming. Maybe she'd been working with girls for too long.

Of course, that apparently wasn't going to be an issue anymore. She squared her shoulders and walked into the kitchen.

Ryder glanced up, his eyes zeroing in on hers. "How'd it go?"

"It didn't. The Shermans still aren't taking my calls."

"I'd stop trying." Ryder had finished doctoring up Benji's eggs, and he pushed the plate back toward the child. "If you keep on, you're only going to look desperate, and that never helps in situations like this."

"I wouldn't know. I've never been in a situation like this before."

"You've never been fired?"

"Have you?"

"A couple of times. Once because my boss felt like I was gunning for his job."

"Were you?"

Ryder grinned. "Yep. In my defense, he was incompetent and a bully. The other time was my fault. I took a big risk, and it didn't pan out."

He glanced up at her, and their eyes connected. Her mind flashed back to the kiss, and suddenly that tickle was back in her stomach again. "Does that happen to you often?"

"My track record with risk-taking is pretty good, but everybody makes an occasional mistake."

She wasn't sure how to take that. "I can take over with the boys now, if you have something else you need to attend to this morning."

"Not particularly. I couldn't sleep last night, so I stayed up and got a little work done. Didn't you say you wanted to check in with Nanny Bev? I can hold down the fort long enough for you to do that, if you'd like to go ahead and make the call."

She did want to. Suddenly the longing to hear Nanny B's familiar voice overwhelmed her. "All right. Thanks. If you're sure you don't mind."

"Not a bit." The smile he offered her was warm, but there was a new hesitancy in his eyes. "We'll probably need to talk some stuff over ourselves later. Don't you think?"

She straightened her shoulders. "Yes, I expect we do."

"Nanny Elise? Why's your face all red?" Benji asked through a second mouthful of eggs.

"Don't talk with your mouth full, kiddo," Ryder said hastily. "Go make your call, Elise, while I try to work on table manners with these two Neanderthals."

Back in the cottage, Elise sighed with relief when Nanny Bev answered on the third ring. The older woman sounded cheerful, at least until Elise explained what had happened. Nanny Bev listened carefully, peppering Elise's explanation with exclamations of dismay.

"Well," she said finally. "If you ask me, you're well rid of them. Of course, it's a pity you didn't have the opportunity to say a proper goodbye to the two girls, but that can't be helped. I wouldn't spend another moment fretting over it if I were you. You'll find a new position quickly, I'm sure. Perhaps your Mr. Montgomery will keep you on. He's been quite pleased with your work, hasn't he?"

Your Mr. Montgomery. Nanny Bev used that sort of wording all the time. She meant nothing by it, but Elise felt her cheeks flame anyway.

"This position was strictly for the summer. The boys are being enrolled in preschool in the fall, and I doubt they'll need a full-time nanny." She walked to the sink, ran a paper towel under cool water and dabbed at her face with it. She really was going to have to get this silly blushing business under control. If a four-year-old was noticing it—

"Well, you never know," Nanny Bev was saying. That unusually chipper note was back in her voice. "Mr. Montgomery's not married, after all."

Elise paused in mid-dab. "What does that have to do with anything?" she asked sharply.

"Only that single parents can benefit from some additional help, even when their children are in school during the day. Elise," Nanny Bev went on, a concerned note creeping into her voice, "has there been some trouble with this Mr. Montgomery that you haven't mentioned to me?"

"No! Nothing like that."

"Good! Well, maybe now that you're free to consider a long-term position, he'll offer one. If not, I'm certain another job will pop up."

"I'm not so sure. The Shermans are unlikely to give me a good reference, and if their reaction is any indication, parents may be reluctant to hire me because of the website. I suppose I could shut it down, but…"

"I wouldn't," Nanny Bev responded firmly. "It's a nice little nest egg for you, and honestly, it sounds like quite a lot of fun."

"It is," Elise agreed. Her mind ticked over the time she'd spent with Torey and Ryder, putting the finishing touches on the site and adding videos. She was no big fan of seeing recordings of herself, although they'd assured her the camera loved her. But the rest of it had been a great deal of fun.

"Then I wouldn't give it up. You could always seek other employment, you know. You've your degree to fall back on."

"Teach, you mean?"

"Why not? You always intended to teach at some point, and you'd still be working with children. It's certainly something to consider. Perhaps you can get a job in that little town. What's its name again?"

"Cedar Ridge?"

"Right. It sounds like a charming place. You've enjoyed being there, haven't you?"

"Yes," Elise answered softly. "Yes, I have, actually."

"Well, then. Perhaps this dismissal is a blessing in disguise—a way for you to stay there. God does some amazing things."

There it was again, that unusual chirpiness in Nanny Bev's voice. "You seem awfully chipper today," Elise said.

"Do I? Well, I didn't want to crow since you've such an unpleasant thing to deal with, but the truth is I've had some very good news."

"Crow away," Elise said. "I could use something to smile about."

"Well, I just got the corner room here. That one with the big windows I've been admiring for so long? The woman who lived in it had to relocate due to the price increase, and it became available. I put in for it, and believe it or not, I got the assignment. I'm moving in tomorrow."

"Oh." Elise's heart sank. Nanny Bev had wanted that particular room for quite some time. If she had to move to a different facility now, she'd be devastated. "That's lovely."

"Isn't it? I do feel bad about profiting from someone else's trouble, of course. So many people are having to leave because of the rate increase." Nanny Bev tsked her tongue sadly. "It makes me feel a bit self-conscious about my own blessings. I mean, it's not everyone who has an anonymous donor helping with her expenses."

"Nanny Bev," Elise said carefully. "I don't want to alarm you, but it might be that your donor won't be able to cover the increase in rates."

"Oh, but he already has, dear."

Elise frowned. "What?"

"I was notified recently that my fees are paid up for the next twelve months. Isn't that wonderful? I believe that's why they gave me the room. I'm guaranteed to be around for a while. Do you know," Nanny Bev went on, a chuckle in her voice, "I did wonder if perhaps you were my anonymous benefactor. You've such a kind heart, and this is just the sort of thing you'd do. It worried me, because I know you haven't the money to spare. So, I'm doubly relieved because, of course, you wouldn't have the sort of money to pay for twelve whole months at a go."

"No," Elise said after a stunned moment. "No, I certainly wouldn't."

"I can't imagine who else would be this kind— or this willing to spend such a large amount of money to help an elderly lady live her last years out in comfort. Whoever it is, he must be quite special."

A bit of movement caught her eye. Ryder was taking the twins out into the yard. Each boy grabbed an arm and dragged their uncle toward their beloved fort. He laughed and allowed himself to be propelled across the yard.

Elise's heart dipped hard.

"Yes," she murmured. "Quite special, indeed."

Chapter Twelve

Ryder sat on the edge of Tuck's twin bed, listening to Elise reading a bedtime story about a frog and a toad. He'd taken over the bedtime routine for the most part, but tonight the twins had talked Elise into participating. She'd agreed, and here they were.

He could have gone downstairs and cracked open his laptop, but he hadn't, even though it was getting harder and harder to find bits of time to sneak in work. The truth was, he hadn't wanted to leave. Right now, Ryder couldn't think of any place in the world he'd rather be.

Outside, a summer storm had blown in, and rain was pattering steadily down. Lightning was flashing in the distance, and thunder rumbled. It was the sort of night that—before he'd come to live with Ruby—had made him hunker down uneasily on his bare mattress—or the back seat of his dad's Dodge, if they happened to be homeless at the time.

But here, inside in the circle of lamplight, everything was cozy and pleasant.

The boys' bedroom was neat, with just enough toys out of place to feel realistic and comfortable. The boys, freshly scrubbed and in their favorite pajamas, sat up in their beds, stuffed dinosaurs tucked carefully under the sheets, absorbed in the story. Elise read expressively, the light behind her gilding her hair, the pages whispering as she turned them, one by one.

He was thankful she was reading tonight. He wasn't sure he could have managed it. Right now he felt like that storybook frog was caught right in the middle of his throat.

When he was a kid, not much older than Tuck and Benji, he remembered being too hungry to sleep and slipping out of the singlewide he and his dad were renting. He'd roamed the trailer park on summer evenings while his father was absorbed in whatever ball game he'd bet on that night. Sometimes Ryder had caught glimpses through windows of scenes like this one, families grouped together around tables with plates of food, or kids snug in beds that looked clean and had sheets.

He hadn't known much about God back then, but he'd known enough to pray that one day he'd have a home like that. One complete with a grown-up who cared, and enough money to stay clean and well-fed. When the foster system had bounced him to Ruby's house, that prayer had been answered.

Now God had answered again. With Elise's help, he'd managed to give his nephews just the kind of home he'd dreamed about as a kid. The relief and gratitude filled his heart so full that it barely fit in his chest.

His eyes were drawn back to Elise's profile, to the way her expression changed depending on what she was reading. He could feel his own expression changing as he watched her.

They hadn't had a chance to talk yet. But they would. That was coming, and he prayed he could find the right way to tell her what he was feeling.

And he'd better pray, because the odds of him getting this right on his own were low. He wasn't even sure what these feelings meant, much less how he could communicate that to Elise.

Guilt. Fear. Joy. Gratitude. All those emotions were mixed up together inside of him, rising up like the bubbles in the twins' bath a little while ago.

But the bubble that popped up the most often—and the biggest one—was hope. That was the one that had his stomach churning, and it had been ever since he'd kissed her.

That kiss marked either the end of something or a brand-new beginning. He couldn't be sure which until he and Elise talked things over, but he knew what he was hoping for.

"And they lived happily ever after," Elise finished in a soothing voice.

Yes, please, God, Ryder prayed silently. *That.*

"Aww. Can we read another story?" Benji pleaded.

"Not tonight," Elise said with a smile. "But tomorrow we can take this book back to the library and get a new one." She shut the book and set it on the bedside table, then helped each boy settle down on their pillows, tucking the sheets up around them with efficient little tugs. "Good night," she said.

"Nanny Elise?"

"Mmm?"

"Our mama…she didn't always feel good at nighttime. But sometimes when she felt good enough to put us to bed, she'd kiss us on our heads."

Elise paused. "She would?"

Both boys nodded, their eyes wide and hopeful.

If Ryder hadn't been watching closely, he might have missed that quick pulse of Elise's neck as she swallowed—and the extra couple of seconds it took her to answer.

"It sounds like she loved you very much," Elise murmured gently.

More nods. And a pause. "You could kiss us on our heads if you wanted to," Tuck offered shyly.

"Yeah. We wouldn't mind," Benji added. "Even though you ain't our mama. We like you."

Ryder's heart crashed into his gut like a seagull after a fish. Looked like he wasn't the only one doing some hoping.

"I like both of you, too," Elise was saying. "Very much." She brushed a kiss over each boy's forehead. When she straightened, she glanced his way. "Maybe your uncle would like a kiss goodnight, too."

Their eyes connected, and she went pink, looking flustered. "I meant—" she started, and he nodded.

"I know."

He'd known what she meant, of course. But somehow, his heart had hammered into high gear anyway.

To cover it, he stepped up and gave each of his nephews a teasingly loud buss on their foreheads. They laughed and protested, and his heart— which he'd thought was already at full capacity—swelled a little more.

They said their good-nights, retrieved one last glass of water for Tucker, then slipped out of the room, leaving the door cracked open so the light in the hallway spilled inside, and so Ryder could hear the boys if they needed anything in the night.

Neither of them spoke until they were back downstairs in the living room. The lightning flashed again, and the thunder rolled not long behind it.

"The storm's getting fierce," Elise said. "I hope it doesn't disturb the boys."

"Doubtful," Ryder said. "Once they doze off, they sleep like logs. Elise, would you have a seat? You and I need to talk."

"All right." She sat on the love seat, and he dropped beside her, leaving a cautious distance between them.

"First off," he said, "I owe you an apology. I shouldn't have kissed you, and I'm sorry I did."

"Oh." Elise blinked, and something flickered in her eyes. It was there and gone so fast that Ryder couldn't be sure, but he was left with the sense that his apology wasn't all that well received. "I see," she ventured after a second or two.

"I hope you do." He took her hands in his. They felt chilly, and he rubbed them gently to warm them. Her eyes widened, but she didn't pull away, which he took as a good sign. "I want to be clear about this. I'm only apologizing for my bad timing, Elise. Right now, you work for me, and for that reason, me kissing you was out of line."

Something flashed in her eyes again, something warmer. "I could have stopped you."

"You could have, but you shouldn't have to. Not under these circumstances. Which leads us to our current problem. The truth is, I'd really like to kiss you again. I'd like to take you out for a nice dinner—just the two of us," he added quickly.

A tiny smile curved her lips. "That would be a change."

"Yeah. It would. But it's one of several changes I'd like to make. If, that is, you'd be interested."

Her eyes were searching his, and her smile bloomed and warmed her face. "I would," she murmured.

He smiled back at her. "Which brings us back to our problem. If we're going to date, then you can't work for me anymore."

She kept her eyes on his and lifted one brow. "Being fired twice in one day wouldn't look very good on my résumé. Maybe I should offer my resignation instead."

"That works for me. Except," he went on carefully, "if you don't work for me, I can't very well keep paying you a salary."

She frowned. "Of course not."

He waited, but she didn't say anything else.

"I understand that money's an issue right now. I don't want to put you in a financial pinch and mess up Nanny Bev's situation, so I have some ideas, if you'd be interested."

She tilted her head. "I talked to Nanny Bev this afternoon. She was in a really good mood."

"That's great to hear." Ryder tried to decipher the expression on her face. She seemed to be trying to tell him something, but he wasn't sure what. "Any particular reason?"

"She'd had some wonderful news." Elise's eyes sparkled at him.

He waited for her to explain, but she didn't. They studied each other for a minute as lightning flickered outside the window. Thunder rumbled, and the tempo of the rain picked up another notch.

"Okay," Ryder said with a short laugh. "I give. I have no idea what we're talking about here. Want to clue me in?"

"Nanny Bev just found out that an anonymous donor had paid for an entire year of expenses at Glen Haven."

"You're kidding! That's incredible. And great timing. Now you won't have to worry about— wait." He frowned. "Elise, I didn't have anything to do with that."

"Ryder—"

"I'm serious. I mean, I wish I had that kind of

money to spare. Trust me, if I did, I'd have been happy to help. But right now, with the company starting up, and the expense of the house, there's no way I could come up with that kind of lump sum on such short notice."

"Oh." Elise leaned back in her seat, her expression puzzled. "But then...who? I can't imagine who else could have done it. I mean, who else would even know about the problem? I haven't talked to anybody but you about it." She shook her head and smiled. "You haven't discussed it with anybody, have you? Maybe some wealthy millionaire friend with a soft spot for elderly nannies?"

Ryder had figured out what had happened before she'd finished speaking, but it took him another couple of seconds to tell her.

"Your father," he said.

Her warm expression chilled so fast it felt like a blow. "What?"

"I mentioned the situation to your dad. I think he sent the money, Elise."

A second ago, sitting here with Ryder in this room had felt...wonderful. The storm outside had only made things cozier. Now, all that warmth had been stripped away. She felt cold and sick.

"You've talked to my father?"

"He called me a few days ago."

She couldn't sit this close to him. Not now. She rose and walked a few steps away, her arms crossed protectively over her chest.

"Why didn't you tell me?"

Ryder got to his feet slowly, as if he was afraid she'd run if he made any sudden moves.

"I should have. I'm sorry."

"That doesn't answer my question."

"It wasn't intentional. Just bad timing. He called the day Ask a Nanny took off. I know the two of you have a complicated relationship, and I didn't want to upset you. I figured I'd wait until after the party, but then…"

"Then the Shermans fired me." An idea occurred to her, and she frowned. "I wonder if he was behind that, too. It wouldn't surprise me a bit."

Ryder shook his head. "I doubt it. He seemed pretty sure you'd be going back to work for the Shermans at the end of the summer. He wasn't happy about it, but he obviously thought that's what was going to happen."

Sounded like they'd had quite the conversation. Elise was still trying to think this through. "But why would my father call you?"

"He said he was worried about you."

Elise bit down on the inside of her cheek. Ryder made this sound so innocent, but she knew her father—which meant she knew better. "How did he even find out I was working for you?"

"He didn't say, but based on some remarks he made, my guess would be he hired a private investigator."

"He did what?" Her initial surprise subsided fast, replaced by a dull, seething certainty. It was exactly the sort of over-the-top, invasive thing her father would do.

Ryder was studying her, his forehead crinkled. "I don't blame you for being upset. But if it makes you feel any better, I think his snooping was mostly focused on me."

"On you?" The bewildered uncertainty she was feeling shifted slightly—very slightly—toward embarrassment. "I'm sorry, Ryder. That was a terrible invasion of your privacy."

He shook his head. "It didn't bother me too much. I have nothing to hide. It was actually the one thing in the conversation I understood. He didn't know where you were or who you were with. If I had a daughter, and she was spending a lot of time with some guy I'd never laid eyes on, I'd probably want to know something about him, too."

"So you'd *ask*." Elise made a disgusted sound. "You wouldn't pay somebody to follow the man around and poke into his life. I'm not a runaway teenager. I'm an adult and perfectly capable of looking after myself. I'd better call him," she decided. She didn't relish the prospect, but she needed to find out exactly what her dad was up to.

Because he was definitely up to something. He always was. Andrew Cooper made no uncalculated moves.

"Sounds like a good first step. Maybe you two can come to some sort of understanding."

She raised an eyebrow. An understanding? With Andrew Cooper? Ha. Elise shook her head. "Unlikely. My father never compromises. When he negotiates, he's more the scorch and burn type."

Ryder hesitated, and she could sense him weighing his words carefully. "This isn't really any of my business. And yeah, I'd say your dad is definitely a hard case. A lot of powerful men are. But I'm pretty good at reading people, and from what I could tell, you have a lot more leverage with him than you might think. You're his soft spot. I think he really cares about you. I know he's way out of line—"

"The way my father sees it, there aren't any lines," Elise interrupted shortly. "Except those he draws himself."

"This is really none of my business," Ryder repeated.

She tilted her chin up a notch. "You're right. You don't know my father."

"No, I don't, but I knew mine. If my dad had

ever showed the least bit of interest in me or my sister…if he'd cared at all what happened to either of us…" Ryder stopped and shook his head. "Things might have gone a lot differently. But he didn't care enough to feed us, much less hire a private investigator to make sure we were safe. And my dad wasn't even as bad as others I know about." His face went grim, and there was a fierce sorrow in his expression that she hadn't seen before. "Some of my brothers and sisters can tell stories a lot worse than mine. Your dad isn't expressing it the right way, there's no doubt about that. But at least he cares about you. Maybe that's something you can build on somehow."

"I appreciate what you're saying, but you still don't understand. There's more than one way to be a bad father. You have no idea the boundaries my dad has trampled over the years, the lengths he's gone to." She made a frustrated noise. "Trust me, as bad as this situation is, it could have been a lot worse. If you were a different kind of man, he'd have offered you some kind of career boost to marry me just so I'd stop embarrassing him by working as a nanny."

Ryder's face shifted, and her heart sank.

Silence held between them for one painful second.

"He did," Elise said quietly. "Didn't he?" And Ryder hadn't told her about it.

This was starting to feel awfully familiar.

"What difference does it make if he did? Trust me, I shut that offer down fast."

Trust me. The pain in her heart was so excruciating, it took her a minute to answer him. "Too bad." Her voice shook with feeling. "He wasn't bluffing. He rewards people who do what he wants. Handsomely. He could have made your sales consultant business a roaring success."

"I don't need his help to do that. Look, you're upset, and I'm really sorry. Why don't we sit down and try to talk this through?"

"I think we've talked enough." She started for the door.

"Elise, please. It's pouring out there." As if to back up his protest, lightning flashed, followed by a roll of thunder. "These summer storms never last long. Just wait a few minutes, and the worst will pass."

She turned to face him, one hand on the doorknob. "Actually, I think this particular storm's settled in to stay a while." Before he could answer, she opened the door and hurried out into the driving rain.

She was drenched before she made it to the cottage's porch. When she glanced back at the house, Ryder stood silhouetted in the kitchen doorway. He'd watched until she made it safely across the yard.

She turned away, determined not to feel touched. If her father had taught her anything, it was that overprotectiveness could become a real problem.

She quickly toweled off and changed into yoga pants and a soft T-shirt, bundling her wet hair up in a towel. Then she sat down on the sofa and grabbed her phone.

She didn't want to do this. She really didn't. But since her father was now involved in Nanny Bev's financial situation, she had to.

She took a deep, steadying breath and started the call.

Her father was never far away from his phone, but he let it ring five times before he answered. Another power play.

"Elise. So good to finally hear from you." There was a slight emphasis on the word *finally*. "All going well, I hope?"

"Hello, Dad. I'd think you'd know exactly how things are going, seeing as how you've had one of your guys here poking around."

"Ah." A chuckle. "I see Ryder has come clean about our little chat. That took a bit longer than I thought it would. You left me no choice, my dear. Apparently that's the sort of tactic I have to resort to if I want to know what's going on in your life."

Was she imagining it, or was there a note of

regret in her father's voice? Nonsense, she told herself. Andrew Cooper didn't believe in regret.

He also didn't believe in charity, not without some underlying motive. Time to get to the purpose of this call.

"Did you pay Nanny Bev's assisted living fees?"

"Did someone do that? Seems a very generous thing to do. Why would you think it was me?"

"Was it?"

"I'm assuming the donation was anonymous or you wouldn't be asking. If her benefactor wants to remain unknown, maybe you should respect that. Besides, I'd think you'd be relieved. It was my understanding from my chat with Mr. Montgomery that your old nanny's financial situation was quite a burden on you."

"Nanny Bev has never been a burden to me."

"Forgive my poor choice of words. But the fact remains, with that cost taken care of, your own financial situation must be considerably improved."

Yes, he'd done it. The satisfaction in his voice gave him away. And her father never handed out anything—particularly not money—unless there were some serious strings attached.

"Why would you do such a thing?"

"I haven't said I did. In any case, I'd expect that would be the least of your concerns just now. I hear you've fallen out of favor with the Shermans."

"Did you have something to do with that, too?"

She'd expected another chuckle and a dodge, but this time her father surprised her. "I did not." He sounded a bit irritated. "In fact, I've made it clear to Jon Sherman that I don't appreciate his decision. Not," he went on swiftly, "that I ever approved of you being in the man's employ in the first place. Still, the idea of him firing my daughter is ridiculous. However, as it happens, things may have worked out for the best."

She frowned. "What do you mean?"

"Well, you don't need the money now, and you appear to be quite happy where you are."

She had been. A lump rose up in her throat.

"Since when does my happiness matter to you?"

"Now you're the one being ridiculous. Your happiness has always been a priority for me. At least we finally seem to be on the same page, you and I. I admit I wasn't delighted when you took this summer job in the boondocks of Georgia. However, I'm willing to confess a mistake when I make one. As I told Ryder during our conversation, his breeding leaves something to be desired, but there's no fault to be found in his intelligence, nor in his business savvy. And believe me, I looked."

Her heartbeat sped up. "Why would Ryder's family situation interest you?"

"I find it useful to know about the personal

lives of my business associates. And Ryder is a special case."

Elise frowned. "How so?"

"No need to be coy, my dear. As it happens, in this case, you have my blessing. Opinions seem to be unanimous. The man's ambitious and smart, and the consensus is that he has a very promising future ahead of him." Another chuckle. "In fact, several of my business associates have mentioned that he reminds them of me when I was young."

"What?"

"Oh, come now. That's not so surprising. They say a daughter often chooses a husband similar to her father, whether she's aware of it or not. The family background is far from ideal, but we can work around that. As I mentioned to Ryder, a self-made man inspires a great deal of admiration, and—"

"You discussed all this with him?" Ryder certainly hadn't told her everything.

"At length." A brief, irritated pause. Her father didn't like being interrupted. "Don't worry. I was quite complimentary."

She was sure that was true. Her father had flattery down to an art form. Most people found him very difficult to resist, particularly when he paired his compliments with enticing promises, as he'd apparently done with Ryder.

Ryder had said he wasn't interested in her

father's offers. But she couldn't forget one extremely obvious point.

The very next day, he'd crossed the lines they'd drawn so carefully and kissed her—and made it clear he was interested in a personal relationship.

Was she supposed to believe that was a coincidence?

She blinked back a hot rush of tears. "I have to go now."

"Wait, Elise. I'd like to see you before the summer's over, and I want to meet Ryder in person. Why don't you bring him home for a long weekend? I could introduce him around, help him make some contacts, get him on everyone's radar. It would be a good first step."

"That's not going to be possible."

Her father made an annoyed noise. "Why not?"

"I've resigned my post here effective immediately, and I doubt I'll be seeing Ryder Montgomery again."

"Elise—"

"Goodbye, Dad." She disconnected the call with a click, then sat there for a minute, her heart beating hard.

She should have seen this coming. She wasn't sure why she hadn't.

No, that wasn't true. She knew exactly why she hadn't seen it. She hadn't wanted to.

She'd desperately wanted to believe Ryder was

different, that all the little similarities she'd noticed between him and her dad—the importance placed on money, the drive, the charm—didn't mean anything.

But they did. Of course they did.

A flash of lightning was followed instantly by a boom of thunder that made the walls of the cottage shudder. The storm was directly overhead now. Elise looked out the window just as Ryder turned off the kitchen light and the house went dark.

Elise stared into the empty blackness for a minute. Then she laid her head on her arms and wept.

Chapter Thirteen

The next afternoon, Ryder stood in the yard watching Elise say goodbye to two bewildered and unhappy twins. It was a flawless summer day—and he felt as if his heart was being gouged out of his chest with a spoon.

He was still struggling to wrap his mind around how everything had shifted sideways. The night before, there had been wind and rain and thunder outside—but peace and hope inside.

Now all that was reversed. The weather was perfect, and the world had a fresh, just-washed feeling to it.

And inside he was a complete wreck.

This was his fault—all of it. He hadn't put all the pieces of this disaster together yet, but that much he knew already.

He'd tried to talk to her, to explain, to apologize. He'd gotten nowhere. She'd retreated behind a firm, professional wall, and none of his powers of persuasion had been a match for it.

In fact, the harder he tried, the more suspicious and distant she'd looked. So, in the end, he'd given up.

The boys looked as devastated as he felt, and the cool facade Elise had kept up all day had slipped as well.

"You're goin' where?" Tucker asked for the third time.

"To England to visit the woman who was my nanny for many years." Elise ruffled the boys' hair gently. "I know this feels very sudden, and I'm terribly sorry about that. It—" She glanced at Ryder and then quickly away. "It couldn't be helped. But I'm going to write to you and send you special packages in the mail. So be on the lookout for those."

"We like gettin' stuff in the mail. But we'd rather have you." Tucker nudged a rock with the tip of his tennis shoe.

Elise's lips trembled, but she smiled. "I'd rather have you, too, but I've promised Nanny Bev a visit, and it's been nearly two years since I've seen her."

"Two years is a real long time," Benji observed solemnly. "She's probably been missing you."

"I think she has. And I've been missing her, too." Elise straightened and smiled. "And of course, I was only supposed to be here for a short time. You'll be going to pre-K soon, and that will be such fun! Now, then. One last hug apiece, please, and then go stand on the porch so I can see you waving as I drive away. And here—" She pulled the miniature flags from her counter out of her shoulder bag and handed one to each child. "These are yours now."

The boys looked at each other, then back at Elise. "For keeps?"

"For keeps. And every time you look at them, you can remember all the happy things about our time together."

"Thank you, Nanny Elise!" they chorused, fluttering the flags enthusiastically.

Ryder felt a twinge of envy. He wished he could cheer up that easily.

"You're quite welcome. Now, off you go to the porch!"

Elise sounded very professional and very chipper, but she wasn't fooling him. He could hear the wobble in her voice. She didn't want to leave the twins any more than they wanted to see her go.

As soon as they were safely on the porch, she turned to him. The warmth faded from her face, replaced by a chilly professionalism.

"They'll have a hard time with this. Change is difficult, and the loss of another female caregiver is going to remind them of…of their mother." Her voice cracked, and she cleared her throat. "I'm so very sorry. I shouldn't have let them grow so attached to me."

"I don't think you could have helped that."

She went on as if she hadn't heard him. "And this abrupt leaving isn't going to help."

"Then don't leave abruptly. Elise, please stay. We should talk—"

She'd cut him off every time he'd tried to open this conversation, and she did the same thing now. "No." She shook her head. "I've already bought my ticket. It's nonrefundable."

"I'd offer to reimburse you for it, but I have a feeling that's not going to get me anywhere."

For a second, he thought he saw a glimmer of humor in her eyes, but it faded quickly. "No, I'm afraid not."

For a long, last second, they looked at each other.

He had to try. Just one more time. "Elise—"

"Goodbye, Ryder." She held out her hand, just as she had the day they'd met in front of the library. "I wish you all the best."

As his fingers closed over hers, for one desperate instant, he wanted to hang on to her. To find some way to make her listen.

Instead, he gave her hand a gentle squeeze and released it. "Thank you, Elise, for all you've done for me and for the boys. If there's ever anything I can do for you—"

She smiled stiffly. "Just deposit my last pay-check, and we'll consider ourselves even."

"I will. But we won't be even."

She tilted her head and offered him another tight-lipped smile. Then she turned to climb into her car. A few seconds later, she was tooting the horn cheerfully and waving as the boys wagged their flags furiously from the porch.

Ryder watched her go, feeling as if his heart was being pulled after her like putty. The boys came off the porch toward him, flags drooping. They looked as dejected as he felt.

"Now what do we do?" Benji asked morosely.

For a second, Ryder didn't know how to answer. Then suddenly he did.

He'd go where he always went when life decked him—to the person who always knew what to say.

And what not to.

"We're going to go visit Grandma Ruby."

Ruby welcomed them with open arms and knew within thirty seconds that something was wrong. She shooed the boys out to pester her goats and chickens and settled Ryder on the back porch with a glass of iced tea. She listened as he filled her in on what had happened, clucking her tongue and shaking her head.

"So," she said with a wry chuckle. "You ran the poor girl all the way to England, did you? That's got to be some kind of record."

"Apparently."

"She coming back?"

"I doubt it."

"You all right with that?"

No. He wasn't all right with that. "I guess I'll have to be."

Ruby snorted. "I raised you better than that, son. Now's not the time to get all pitiful."

He pulled his gaze away from the boys, who were having a standoff with Ruby's stubborn billy goat, and shifted in the rocking chair to face his foster mom. He'd expected sympathy, but he saw nothing but challenge in Ruby's wrinkled face. "What?"

"I really got to spell this out for you?" Ruby leaned forward. "You need to go after her."

"It wouldn't do any good, Ruby. She doesn't want anything to do with me. She made that very clear."

"'Course she did." Ruby waited, but when he just stared, she made another annoyed noise. "Didn't you learn nothing from growing up in this house?"

"Apparently not. I don't have a clue what you're talking about."

Ruby shot him an exasperated look. "What time does her plane leave?"

"At seven, I think." He was only pretending to be vague. He knew exactly what time, and what airline, and he'd even looked up the flight number on their website.

Ruby checked her scratched wristwatch. "We're gonna have to make this quick. You in love with her or not?"

"Ruby—"

"We ain't got time to dance around, son. It's a yes or no question."

He studied the tiny woman in front of him. Fine. "Yeah."

Relief—and maternal annoyance—flickered across Ruby's face. "'Yes, ma'am' would be better."

"Yes, ma'am, then. I love her. Not that it matters."

Another exasperated snort. "Of course it matters, son. Love's the only thing that ever matters."

"Not if the other person doesn't love you back."

Another snort. "What makes you think she doesn't?"

Now she had his undivided attention. "She's sure not acting like it."

"She's acting exactly like it. Why's she going all the way to England? To get as far away from you as she can 'cause you've hurt her feelings. If that ain't a woman in love, I don't know what is."

"Ruby, you're not making sense." She wasn't, but a flicker of hope stirred to life anyway.

"Oh, I'm talking sense, all right. You just can't think about nothing right now except that ache in your chest. Son, you've seen this a thousand times before in this very house. This is what happens when you bump up against somebody's scars. And the more that person cares about you, the more pain it causes."

Ryder knew what Ruby was referring to. His foster siblings had tough histories, and all of them had wounds. Growing up, they'd tried to respect each other's sore spots, but of course they'd messed up from time to time. Some of the reactions had been epic, and the person who'd caused the hurt was always remorseful.

Eventually.

The kids who'd ended up at Ruby's had experienced too much pain to ever want to cause it in others.

It made him squirm to think he'd hurt Elise like that, but he wasn't convinced he had. "It's not the same thing. Elise doesn't come from a background like ours. She grew up with everything. Money, education, attention. She doesn't have the kind of scars we have."

"Son, you're being as thick as a plank." Ruby shook her head. "Sounds to me like when you went behind her back and spoke with her daddy, you bumped a real sore spot. You know better than most how tough relationships with a parent can be."

Well, yes, he did. "Elise's situation is different. Her father's self-centered and manipulative, sure. But deep down, he cares about his daughter."

"Oh, for pity's sake. People can care a whole lot and still stomp all over each other's hearts. When love gets twisted out of shape, it causes all sorts of problems. Sounds like that's been going on for years with Elise and her father. It's hard for a man to raise a little girl without a mama, for one thing. And this Mr. Cooper sounds like he's pretty tone-deaf about folks' feelings. Kind of like somebody else I know," Ruby muttered. "Buying dishwashers and such-like."

"For the ten-thousandth time, I was wrong about the dishwasher, but this wasn't my fault. I didn't call Andrew Cooper, Ruby. He called me."

"That part wasn't your fault, maybe. But you knew she and her father were on the outs. You still didn't tell her that he'd called you—not until you had to. And when you did, you didn't tell her everything until she picked it out of you."

"That was just the timing, Ruby. I was going to tell her."

"Go sell that snake oil someplace else." Ruby studied him with that no-nonsense look he knew so well. "You didn't tell her because first off, you were afraid she'd be upset, and you'd started having some pretty big feelings for her."

Ryder hesitated. "All right. I'll admit that much."

"Don't get comfortable, 'cause the second reason's worse. You didn't tell her because deep down, you don't think she's got good reason to be mad at her father."

"That's not true."

"Ain't it? You said as much to me just now. You'd never had kept such a secret from one of your brothers and sisters, not for five minutes. 'Course not. You know the kind of pain it causes when someone you trust goes behind your back to talk to somebody you don't trust as far as you can spit. You been taking it for granted that any girl born with a silver spoon in her mouth couldn't have had as bad a time growing up as you did. And you're wrong. Pain is pain, son, and money don't make near as much difference as you think it does. If you think it through, you'll see that." She glanced at her wristwatch again. "But you'll have to do your thinking in the car. If you plan on apologizing before she hightails it to England, you'd better get yourself to that airport."

Ryder hesitated, then glanced at his own watch. He might be able to catch her before she went through security.

Possibly.

He wasn't sure it would do any good, and he

still wasn't sure Ruby was right. But, he realized, he didn't care.

He wanted to try anyway.

"Will you watch the boys?"

"'Course I will. They're hardly any trouble nowadays, thanks to Elise. Another reason to go after her. Now, scoot! You know how that Atlanta traffic is. You got no time to waste."

Before she finished the sentence, Ryder was jogging across the yard to his car.

Ruby was right about the traffic, and the Atlanta airport was on the south side of the city, so he had to fight his way through downtown. By the time he reached the airport and found parking, he was cutting it close.

He sprinted into the international terminal and looked for the check-in line for Elise's airline. There were only about twenty people in it—and Elise wasn't one of them.

Strike one.

He headed for the security screening area. He scanned the crowd as he went, hoping against hope he'd catch sight of her, but he didn't.

Strike two.

The airport official checking tickets and identification glanced up as he approached the entrance to the screening area. "Ticket, sir."

"I'm not flying. I'm looking for a friend of mine—"

The uniformed man shook his head. "If you're not flying today, sir, you can't pass this point. I'm sorry. If you need to get a message to your friend, talk to customer service. They may be able to relay a message for you."

Strike three. He shouldn't have been surprised. He'd known catching up with her was a long shot.

But he'd had to risk it.

"Sir?" The guard was looking at him, one eyebrow lifted.

"Sorry. Yeah, I understand. Thanks."

Ryder stepped away, making room for a young family. The dad held out his phone to the guard, displaying the tickets, while his wife knelt to talk to their two rosy-cheeked little girls, who were bouncing with excitement. After they were cleared to enter, the dad reached down, swung one of his daughters up into his arms, and said something to his wife, who laughed and leaned her head against his shoulder.

Ryder swallowed a painful lump of jealousy and glanced at his watch. Not long before her plane boarded. He considered the customer service desk, but there was no way he could say what he had to say in a message.

He needed to talk to Elise face-to-face.

A possibility occurred to him, and he stopped short. Passengers veered past him on either side, looking annoyed. He ignored them, his brain ticking over the new idea. It was a huge risk—and probably a foolish one.

But it was a possibility—the last possibility, and right now he couldn't afford to be picky.

He pulled his cell phone out of his pocket and dialed Ruby's number.

Elise shifted in her seat, trying to keep her elbows off the armrests. She hated middle seats, particularly on lengthy flights. It was only ten minutes since takeoff, and the pilot had just turned off the seat belt sign, but she was already cramped and uncomfortable. However, since this was a last-minute booking, there hadn't been many seats to choose from.

The middle-aged woman on her right glanced up from the romance novel she was reading. "Honey, you can use those armrests. We've each got one of our own."

The crankier-looking woman who had the aisle seat frowned. "I'd appreciate it if you didn't speak for me. I get muscle cramps, and I need to use both armrests."

The nicer woman rolled her eyes. "Since we're going to be sitting beside each other for the next few hours, we'd better get acquainted. I'm Millie."

"Elise." She offered a perfunctory smile, then dropped her eyes to the mystery novel she'd opened on her tablet. She hoped this very pleasant woman wasn't going to try to chat. She didn't want to talk. She didn't want to read, either, but maybe if she pretended to, she could avoid conversation.

"You a nervous flyer?" Millie went on. "You seem like you might be a nervous flyer. Your face is all scrunched up, that's how I can tell. Me, I love to fly. You meet so many nice people."

"A nice person would quit yapping so she could read," the crankier woman muttered.

"Well." Millie sent a pointed glare in the other woman's direction. "You meet *some* nice people."

Elise managed a wobbly smile. "I'm quite used to flying. Thanks for your concern, but I'm fine."

Her voice broke on the fib. She wasn't fine. She was anything but fine.

She just had to get through this flight, she told herself doggedly. Then she'd be in England, and she could go see Nanny Bev. And the first thing she planned to do was bury her face in the older woman's shoulder and cry her heart out.

Then together they'd figure out what to do next. Maybe she could find some way to stay in England. She'd like being closer to Nanny B, and she wouldn't mind having an ocean between herself and her father.

Ryder, too. An image of his face popped up in her memory, and the tears stinging the back of her eyes welled up and spilled over. She fumbled in her purse for a tissue.

Millie beat her to it. "Oh, sweetie. Here." The woman handed her a packet of tissues and patted her arm. "See there, I knew something was wrong. Just couldn't put my finger on what. I have amazing instincts about people. Everybody says so."

The cranky woman snorted and turned a page.

"You want to talk about it?" Millie asked.

"No, not particularly. But thank you."

"Okay." Millie looked disappointed. "You change your mind, let me know. I'm a real good listener, and we've got a long flight ahead of us."

"Getting longer by the minute," the cranky woman muttered.

"There's no need to be rude," Millie said sharply.

"Exactly." The other woman shut her book with a snap. "I never understand why people assume that strangers want to chat on an airplane. Why don't you leave this poor young woman alone, and—"

"Elise?"

She'd slumped in her seat, wishing she'd been seated anyplace else, but at the sound of her name, she jerked upright.

Ryder stood in the aisle, looking down at her.

"Surprise," he said.

Chapter Fourteen

Elise blinked. But when she opened her eyes again, Ryder was still there. Her heart flooded with a confusing rush of joy and pain.

"What…" She fumbled to a stop. "How did you get on this airplane?"

"Same way everybody else did. I bought a ticket."

"You bought a ticket," she repeated.

"I had my passport in the glove compartment of my car. I couldn't catch you before you went through security, so I went back to the counter and bought a ticket."

"But—the twins?"

"Oh, my. Twins?" Millie was leaning forward, listening intently. "You have twins?"

Elise ignored her.

"They're with Ruby. Logan and Charlotte are picking them up this afternoon and keeping them overnight. Excuse me, ma'am?" Ryder turned his attention to the cranky woman. "I need to talk to my friend. Would you mind switching seats with me? I'm in first class."

Elise frowned. "You bought a first-class ticket? At the airport?"

"Last minute, especially after my jog out to the parking lot for my passport. I had to take what I could get."

"Go on," Millie urged the other woman. "Swap seats with him." She shook her head. "This is so romantic, I can hardly stand it."

The cranky woman regarded her coldly. "I've no desire to sit in first class, and I've already stowed my carry-on in the overhead bin above this row." She turned to Ryder. "I'm sorry, but no. I'm not going to exchange seats."

Ryder looked taken aback. "Ma'am, I'm really sorry to trouble you, and I'd be happy to help you move your bag. It would mean a lot if—"

"I said no."

Millie sucked in an outraged breath. "Well, if that ain't the most selfish thing I've ever heard! You want to talk to this fellow, honey?"

Elise swallowed and looked at Ryder. She read the plea in his eyes.

"Yes," she whispered.

"That's all I need to know." The plump woman struggled to her feet, yanking her oversize purse out from under the seat in front of her. "I'll change seats with you, Mister, if this coldhearted biddy will get up and let me out. That ain't too much trouble for you, is it?"

"Not at all." The other woman calmly stood and edged into the aisle.

Elise followed. As she slipped into the narrow aisle, she was barely a foot from Ryder. When he looked into her eyes, all the confused feelings whirling inside her went warm and soft and still.

A few minutes ago, she'd felt cold, empty and miserable. Now everything felt different.

The whole world felt different.

She didn't know why Ryder had done such an unexpected, extravagant thing, or if the talk he wanted to have with her was going to make any difference.

But right now none of that mattered. She was just so glad he was here.

"'Scuse me, honey. I've got to get by," Millie said.

"Oh, of course." Elise stepped backward.

"Thank you so much," Ryder said. "Here's the seat number. If you have any problems, let me know."

"I'm not going to have any problems. Bless you, honey." Millie enveloped Elise in a strongly perfumed hug. "Bless you and him and them twins. I just know everything's going to work out fine. Why, one time my husband and I—"

"Do you *mind*?" The cranky woman huffed behind Elise. "We're standing in the aisle here."

"All *right*. Some people. Honestly." Millie bustled toward the front of the plane, muttering under her breath.

"I'm sorry to inconvenience you," Ryder said politely. "Would you rather have the window seat or stay on the aisle?"

"I'll take the window seat," the cranky woman said. "You take the aisle. Your legs are longer than mine."

After they'd settled back in the row, she glanced at them. "You're welcome, by the way." She leaned forward and lowered her voice. "If I'd agreed to swap, you'd have been stuck with Millie, and you wouldn't have had any hope of carrying on a conversation because she'd have kept butting in. Not much privacy on an airplane, but at least we can do better than *that*." The woman produced a set of headphones from her leather purse and wiggled them. "Noise-canceling. I'm going to put these on, close my eyes and ignore you."

Ryder grinned. "Thanks."

The other woman made a face. "No need. Believe me, sending Millie to first class wasn't an entirely selfless act." She slipped on the headset, angled herself toward the window and opened her book.

Ryder shifted in his seat so he was facing Elise. "We need to talk."

"I can't believe you're here." Her stunned brain struggled to comprehend this whole situation. "Did you bring any luggage?"

"Not even a toothbrush."

"You're flying to England with nothing? Not even…you know…clothes?"

"Nope. I wasn't thinking about any of that. The only thing I could think about was getting to you so I could apologize. I'm sorry, Elise. I should have told you I talked to your father the minute I hung up on him. I know you two have a complicated history, and I shouldn't have waited to tell you about his call."

"No, you shouldn't have, but you've already apologized. I…guess I wasn't very gracious. I just needed some time and…um…space." That last bit seemed a bit ironic since right now they were sitting closer than they ever had.

"I understand. Maybe I should have given you that, but I couldn't wait. The apology's only the start of it. You and I have some really important things to work out."

"But Ryder, a first-class ticket…those things cost an arm and a leg."

"Believe me, I know. And I also know this

might be Ruby's dishwasher all over again, but when I got to that airport, nothing mattered to me but catching up with you. You were my top priority, Elise." He leaned forward, taking her hands in his. "You *are* my top priority. You and the boys. And I promise you, from this point on I'll be one hundred percent on your side. All the time, in everything. That is, if you'll let me."

She swallowed. Seats in economy class were packed together like sardines, but she had a feeling it wouldn't have mattered if they'd been in the middle of the Grand Canyon. The world would still have shrunk down to just the two of them.

He was looking into her eyes, and she knew he was asking her a question. And even though she wasn't sure yet exactly what that question was, she knew what she wanted to say.

Yes.

As he squeezed her hands, she could feel him shaking. "When you came to Cedar Ridge, I said you were an answer to a prayer. We all said that, and we meant it. But I don't think I fully understood then how true that was. God answered my prayers bigger and better than I ever could have imagined."

"He does tend to do that," she whispered.

"My world was falling apart when I met you," he said. "I was about one more four-year-old meltdown from giving up. My whole life was a wreck. Then you walked in, and everything just…"

She couldn't help it. She was hanging on his every word, and she had to know.

"What?"

He freed one hand to touch her cheek. "Everything just came together. I don't know how you did it. I'll probably never know. But somehow you took three people who were coming apart at the seams, and you turned us into a family. That's huge, but this…what's between us, what I feel for you…it's even more than that. You don't just make me a better father, Elise. You make me a better man. Because when I'm with you, I'm…" Ryder made a frustrated noise. "I'm home, Elise. And I don't care how many first-class tickets I have to buy or where I have to go. I never want to let go of that. I never want to let go of you."

Elise's heart pounded in her ears. Oh, she wanted to believe this was possible. She wanted to believe this so much. But no matter how she felt about things, the truth was the truth.

She'd learned that the hard way.

"I don't want to let go, either," she said quietly. "Leaving the boys…and you…was the hardest thing I've ever done. But Ryder, we look at the world so differently, you and I. I just don't think…"

"I thought so too, at first." His hands were

holding hers again—so tightly now that she could barely feel her fingertips. "But, Elise, honestly. I don't think we do. The other night when you were reading to the boys at bedtime while that storm crashed around us—that's what I want. A home full of faith and family...and love...no matter how wild the world gets outside. Isn't that what you want, too?"

Yes. Yes, it was.

But she swallowed, reminding herself sternly of what her father had said, of his praise for Ryder's ambition.

"But money just isn't important to me, Ryder. And it's very important to you."

"Sure it is. It's one way to look after the people I care about. So, yeah, I want to be successful at work. I want enough money to keep a roof overhead and plenty of food on the table. I don't ever—*ever*—want to see my family going without the things they need. But money's just a tool, Elise. You were right. It's not the answer to everything." He paused. "Although I think I've figured out what is—for me, anyway."

"And what would that be?"

For the first time, he smiled, and that one dimple winked her a promise. "We'll get to that. Full disclosure on this deal, Elise. I still want to be rich—really rich in everything that matters. I want to have a home and a family of my own. I want to have the woman I love with me for the rest of my life. And in case you still haven't figured it out, that's you. I love you."

"Oh!" For a second she couldn't think straight enough to answer. A sharp jab of an elbow jarred her back to her senses. She turned, and the cranky woman made a face and nodded toward Ryder.

Say it back, she mouthed.

Those noise-canceling headphones must not work so well after all.

Ryder shook his head. "You don't have to say anything right now. I know I've messed up. And I'll probably mess up again. I'm better at deals than relationships."

He looked so determined, so dogged, that she had to fight a smile. "Is that more full disclosure?"

Maybe he saw the hint of a smile on her face, because some hope sparked into his eyes. "Best way to make any deal you want to last," he assured her. "Be honest. That's Sales 101. So, yeah. Messing up is kind of my specialty when it comes to the people I care most about. I buy stuff I shouldn't…dishwashers, flowers…" He fished in his pocket and held out his hand. "Bracelets." The slender scrap of jewelry sparkled on his palm.

She touched it lightly with a fingertip. "You still have that?"

"I've carried it in my pocket for weeks. Tuck

and I have a lot in common, and this reminds me that when I want to give somebody something beautiful, I'd better slow down and step carefully or I just end up causing trouble. I've needed that reminder because I want to give the boys the best of everything." He stopped and swallowed. "And you. I want to give you the best of everything, too. If it was up to me, I'd give you everything you ever dreamed of."

Elise shook her head. "Ryder—"

"I know. No dishwashers. No over-the-top flower arrangements. Because here's the deal, Elise. What I really want to give you is the best of *me*. And I'm not sure exactly how to do that— or if you'd even be interested. But if you can just find it in your heart to let me try, I promise you, I'll do my best to make sure you never regret it. I'll—"

"That's enough," she interrupted softly. "That's more than enough. I don't expect you to take care of me or provide everything I could ever think of wanting. I don't expect you to be perfect, Ryder. I just want you to be...*you*." She paused and ignored the second jab of an elbow—because she was going to say it anyway. "I love you, too."

"Are you sure? Even after reading all the fine print here?" The desperate hope in his eyes made her heart—what had Ruby called it?

Flutter. A very good word, too. Her heart was

fluttering so hard right now, she expected it to fly out of her chest at any moment.

"Yes." She'd never felt surer of anything in her life. "You have the best heart, Ryder. I've met a lot of people who've done spectacular things, who've been hugely successful. But do you know, I've never met anybody with a heart like yours."

"I'm glad to hear that, because I'm putting it on the table. If you're sure you want it."

"I do."

One corner of his mouth tipped up. "Think you might be willing to seal this deal by saying that again in a few months?"

"That's a distinct possibility."

Hope—mixed with disbelief—shone in his eyes. "Elise, just to be clear so there's no confusion here. I'm asking you to marry me."

"I know that, silly. And I'm saying yes." And she leaned forward and touched her lips to his.

Their kiss was sweet and far too short. The sound of applause broke through her befuddled brain, and she drew back, confused.

Maybe it had seemed as if they were alone in the world, but they definitely weren't. Half the plane was clapping, and people in rows too distant to have heard what was happening were standing up and craning their necks to see what was going on.

"Where's the ring?" a man sitting across the aisle asked. "Got to give the girl a ring."

"I'm sorry." Ryder turned back to her with a wry smile. "I don't have a ring—" The passengers close by began a collective *awww*, and he raised his voice to be heard over it. "*Yet*. I don't have a ring yet. We'll pick one out together in England."

"But you're s'posed to give her *something*." A little girl was peering over the seat in front of them, her eyes wide.

"See?" Ryder shot her a humorous look and sighed. "Already messing up."

"The bracelet," she said suddenly. "Give me the bracelet."

"Seriously?"

"Yes. It's been a reminder to you long enough. Now it'll remind me of the three people I love best in the world."

He grinned and slipped it on her wrist as the plane broke out into another round of applause. He leaned in close to whisper in her ear.

"That's a placeholder. I'm buying you a ring the minute we touch down in England. Non-negotiable."

"All right. But," she added quickly, "not an expensive one. Also non-negotiable."

"Fine. We can go poking around in junk shops and buy one secondhand. I'll get you the cheapest ring in the store if that's what you want. But there's one condition."

"What?"

"That you wear it for the rest of your life."

"Ryder Montgomery," she said, throwing her arms around his neck, "you have yourself a deal."

Epilogue

The church's bridal room was jammed with women. Ruby, Charlotte, Torey, Maggie and Jina, Ryder's youngest foster sister, peered around Elise's shoulders, studying her reflection in the full-length mirror.

"Oh, please say something." Charlotte was directing the wedding, and she'd designed the dress herself. "Do you like it?"

"How can you even ask?" Elise barely recognized herself. The A-line dress was a rich, creamy satin, overlaid with delicate lace. It was elegant in its simplicity and absolutely perfect. "I love it!"

"Oh-I'm-so-glad." Charlotte breathed the sentence out as one word, her face relaxing with relief. "You said so at the fittings, but you never know how a dress will suit a bride until the wedding day when she sees it in context."

In context. Elise smiled at the mirror. Charlotte shouldn't have worried. The other women clustered around her, the younger four dressed in bridesmaid dresses of varying styles, all in a shade Charlotte had called "dusty burgundy." Perfect, she'd assured Charlotte, for a wedding in early December.

"You're pretty as a picture." Ruby had chosen a silver-gray dress, bought off the rack but adapted by Charlotte's nimble fingers to suit her mother-in-law's spare frame. "The dress suits you real well, and I know just what it needs to finish it off. I got a little wedding present for you."

"You already gave us our gift," Elise reminded her. "The memory quilt." It had turned out beautifully, and she'd insisted on having it displayed in the reception hall.

"That was for you and Ryder both. This here is just for you." She reached up and unhooked the clasp of the pearl necklace she was wearing, then stepped behind Elise and draped it around her neck. "There, now. Perfect."

Astonished and touched, Elise reached up to caress the warm pearls. "Oh, Ruby!"

"Ryder gave me those." The older woman squinted through her bifocals, fiddling with the tiny clasp. "Bought 'em with his first paycheck. I fussed him out good for wasting the money, let me tell you. But he says to me, 'Ruby, if a fellow can't buy the woman he loves best a string of pearls, what good is havin' money?'" She finished fastening the necklace and gave it a satisfied pat. "I ain't that woman now, honey, much as he'll always love me. So these should pass to you."

"Oh, *Ruby*," Elise repeated, her voice breaking. She wasn't the only one. All the women around her sniffled—except for Torey, who rolled her eyes.

"Here we go," she muttered. "I knew there was going to be crying."

"Group hug," Maggie announced in a wobbly voice. Elise felt their arms going around her, felt the warm squeezes as each one pressed close. She looked at the mirror again, at the picture they made—her sisters, her new mother, surrounding her with their love and friendship.

Along with Ryder and the twins, these people were her family.

That did it. The tears spilled over.

Torey gave a long-suffering sigh. "It's a good thing I know how silly you all are at weddings." She rummaged in her bag, producing a big box of tissues.

As the women took turns plucking tissues from the box, Ruby shot her foster daughter a loaded look.

"Just you wait until your turn, Torey, and we'll see how silly you think all this is."

Torey snorted. "You'll ruin your batting average if you try to match me up, Ruby. Better move on to Nick, since he's the only unmarried brother left. Or Jina here."

Jina looked alarmed. "Hey! Don't throw me under the bus."

"Somebody better change the subject," Maggie murmured. "Fast."

"Elise, I called my friend in Savannah this morning," Charlotte interjected desperately. "And double checked your reservation. You're going to love the Whitefield Inn. It's got the most sought-after honeymoon suite in town."

"I believe you. They're booked a year and a half out. We'd never have gotten in if you hadn't called in a favor."

Jina shook her head. "I still don't see why you and Ryder didn't take your dad up on his offer of a trip to Italy. I mean, Savannah's nice enough, but it can't compete with a two-week honeymoon in Tuscany."

"We didn't want to be that far from the twins for so long," Elise said.

That was true, but it was only part of the reason they'd turned down her dad's offer. She and Ryder considered it wise to establish firm boundaries with Andrew Cooper right from the start. Progress was slow, but her father was coming around.

Maggie chuckled. "When I went out to check the cake, the boys were begging Ryder to take them along on the honeymoon. Your father was promising them a trip to the toy store if they'd hush."

"Oh, no."

"Now, don't fuss," Ruby said. "I know your daddy's too free with his money, but he's gonna be their grandpa, ain't he? Spoiling comes with that territory. You'll have plenty of time to reel him in later."

Andrew Cooper, a grandpa. Elise still couldn't quite wrap her head around that. "I suppose you're right."

"I'm real glad you agreed to let him give you away." Ruby patted Elise's arm. "In my experience, families require a lot of forgiveness, so it's just as well you're starting yours off with a big helping of it."

"I want to check on the cake one last time." Maggie cast a worried glance at her watch.

"We'll all go," Ruby decided. "Elise might like a minute alone before this shindig gets going. Prayer's another good way to start off a marriage," she advised Elise with a wink.

Alone in the room, Elise lifted her left hand and wiggled her finger. The old-fashioned engagement ring she and Ryder had found in a London antique shop twinkled at her. She smiled and bowed her head.

Thank You, Lord, for turning a disappointment into the best thing that ever happened to me. For leading me to the one You set apart for me. For bringing me home and surrounding me with people who are so easy to love. Help me to—

"Hey!"

Startled, Elise opened her eyes. She glanced in the mirror in time to see Tucker and Benji flinging open the door and tearing into the dressing room.

"Guess what? There's a big surprise!"

"I think," Elise said dryly, "that we may need another lesson in knocking."

The twins, dressed in matching gray suits, were barreling toward Elise at full speed, but when she turned around, they stopped short. Both boys stared up at her, their eyes round.

"Wow," Benji breathed.

"You don't look like you," Tucker said.

"She sure don't," Benji agreed. "She's *pretty*."

Elise laughed. "Come here." She sank to their level and held out her arms. "Give me a hug, both of you."

They crowded close and she scrunched them in, breathing in their wonderful little-boy scent. She would get to mother these two, and that prospect gave her so much joy. She couldn't help it. She sniffled again.

Good thing Torey had left the room.

Benji drew back and frowned. "Why you cryin', Nanny Elise?"

"*Aunt* Elise," Tucker corrected him.

"I'm just very, very happy," she said.

"You're going to be even happier," Benji announced. "Because Uncle Ryder's got you a great big surprise."

"He does?"

"Yeah—it's—"

"A secret." She looked up to find Ryder standing in the doorway, looking exasperated—and incredibly handsome. The gray suit he was wearing set off his dark hair—and his shoulders.

He had his hand over his eyes. "I'm not looking. I know I'm not supposed to see the bride before the wedding. Besides, I have a feeling if I take one look at you, I won't be able to stop looking until you're safely my wife. You'd better shoo our runaway ring bearers in my direction."

"First tell me about this secret you've been keeping."

"It cost a lotta money," Tucker informed her solemnly.

"Tuck! Not one more word." Ryder beckoned with his free hand. "Come on!"

"Wait, Uncle Ryder. I got you a present too,

Nanny… I mean Aunt Elise," Tucker announced. He dug in his pocket and produced a slightly smushed sugar rose.

"You stoled that off Aunt Mags's cake," Benji said disapprovingly.

"It's not stealing! The cake's for everybody, and Aunt Maggie promised I could have a piece with a rose. I just took it early, that's all."

Elise fought to keep her face straight as he laid the sticky prize gently in her palm. Somewhere in the reception hall, Maggie was frantically doing damage control. "Thank you."

"Come *on*, boys."

The boys trudged in his direction. As he turned away, Elise called after him.

"Ryder? About this secret—buying the house was our wedding present to each other." She still couldn't believe that. The beautiful little home— including the boys' beloved fort—was officially theirs. "That was our deal."

"Well, technically this gift is only on loan. Ruby's bringing it now. You can let me know if you want it returned."

He stepped out of the doorway, and Ruby appeared, supporting a frail, elderly woman with one arm. Elise took one look and rushed toward them.

"Nanny Bev!"

"Don't knock her over, now," Ruby chided

gently as Elise enveloped her old nanny in a big hug. "She's had a real long trip. She was supposed to be here yesterday, but her flight got delayed cause of bad weather. Ryder's been nervous as a cat in a rocking chair factory, fretting over whether she'd get here in time. But our Nick drove to the airport to get her, and here she is, safe and sound."

"Just in time for your wedding, dear girl," Nanny Bev said happily. "And I'll be staying with this delightful lady while you and your new husband are off on your honeymoon, so I can spend a bit of time with you when you come back. I'll be here a whole month. Isn't that lovely? Your young man arranged it all. This is an answer to my prayers!"

Ruby shot her a speculative look. "You're a praying woman, are you?"

"I certainly am."

"You like to sew?"

"I've been known to thread a needle in my day."

"I got a brand-new quilt I'm about to start on. It's for my girl Torey. You can help me with it, maybe."

"Sounds delightful."

Elise smothered a smile. They hadn't even finished this wedding yet, and Ruby was already working on the next one. Torey had better stock up on tissues.

She gave Nanny Bev one long squeeze. Then she gathered up her dress and ran to where Ryder was standing, his back to the room.

"Ryder," she murmured, reaching up a hand to touch his shoulder. "I don't mind if you see me a little early. Turn around. Please."

He hesitated only a moment, then turned.

His eyes went wide, then darkened. "Breathtaking," he murmured.

"Thank you," she whispered.

He smiled. And leaned in close.

"Aaank!" Ruby swatted him. "Lookin's one thing. Kissing's got to wait until you're standing at the altar."

"Logan!" Charlotte's frantic voice called up the hallway. "What's Ryder doing here? You're supposed to be keeping track of him." She appeared in the doorway and shook her finger at them. "If you two changed your mind about a first look, you should have let me know. I would have gotten the photographer. Maggie's got some emergency about the cake, but Torey's dragging her back because the ceremony's about to start. Ruby, you need to go to the front of the church. You'll be seated as the mother of the groom. And Nanny Bev, we're going to seat you at the same time, as the bride's special person."

"Oh, my." Nanny Bev shook her head. "You're going to make me cry."

"And you. Out." Charlotte tugged at Ryder's coat sleeve. "You two have the rest of your lives to stare into each other's eyes. Right now your wedding's in fifteen—no, ten minutes!"

Elise couldn't seem to pull her gaze away from Ryder's. *I love you*, she mouthed.

He grinned. "All things considered," he murmured, "I certainly hope so."

"Logan? Take him where he's supposed to be."

Her husband appeared. "We've got our orders. Come on."

"I love you, too," Ryder got out before he was dragged away. "See you in a few minutes," he called, looking over his shoulder. "And when I do, I'm claiming my kiss."

Elise smiled as her bridesmaids—who in only a few minutes would officially become her sisters—crowded back around her.

"I'm holding you to that," she promised.

The last thing she saw before Logan hustled her soon-to-be husband out of sight was the flash of a solitary dimple.

* * * * *

Dear Reader,

Welcome back to Cedar Ridge, Georgia! I'm so glad you've come along for my third trip to this sweet small town, nestled in the beautiful Blue Ridge mountains!

If this is your first visit, then you're in for a treat. You're about to meet Ruby Sawyer! This heart-of-gold foster mom is one of my all time favorite characters.

Dedicated foster parents like Ruby are often unsung heroes. They make such an incredible difference in children's lives. Ruby has certainly made a difference to her six foster kids. And even though they're all grown up, Ruby's not done yet. She's determined to see them all get their very own happily-ever-afters.

Ruby's a combination of so many women I've personally admired over the years—the plain spoken, faith-filled ladies who follow the Lord's nudging to get to work wherever they see a need. What a blessing they are! Where would the world be without them?

From chatting with my readers, I know that many of you are much like Ruby. Like her, you serve those around you selflessly—meeting needs and comforting hurting hearts. You inspire me so much!

I'd love to stay in touch! Head over to www.laurelblountbooks.com and join my beloved newsletter subscribers! Every month, I share photos, giveaways, book news and gotta-try-it recipes. And of course, you can always write to me at laurelblountwrites@gmail.com. I look forward to hearing from you!

Much love,
Laurel

Get 4 FREE REWARDS!

We'll send you 2 FREE Books plus 2 FREE Mystery Gifts.

FREE Value Over **$20**

Both the **Love Inspired®** and **Love Inspired® Suspense** series feature compelling novels filled with inspirational romance, faith, forgiveness and hope.

YES! Please send me 2 FREE novels from the Love Inspired or Love Inspired Suspense series and my 2 FREE gifts (gifts are worth about $10 retail). After receiving them, if I don't wish to receive any more books, I can return the shipping statement marked "cancel." If I don't cancel, I will receive 6 brand-new Love Inspired Larger-Print books or Love Inspired Suspense Larger-Print books every month and be billed just $6.49 each in the U.S. or $6.74 each in Canada. That is a savings of at least 16% off the cover price. It's quite a bargain! Shipping and handling is just 50¢ per book in the U.S. and $1.25 per book in Canada.* I understand that accepting the 2 free books and gifts places me under no obligation to buy anything. I can always return a shipment and cancel at any time by calling the number below. The free books and gifts are mine to keep no matter what I decide.

Choose one: ☐ **Love Inspired**
Larger-Print
(122/322 IDN GRHK)

☐ **Love Inspired Suspense**
Larger-Print
(107/307 IDN GRHK)

Name (please print)

Address   Apt. #

City   State/Province   Zip/Postal Code

Email: Please check this box ☐ if you would like to receive newsletters and promotional emails from Harlequin Enterprises ULC and its affiliates. You can unsubscribe anytime.

Mail to the Harlequin Reader Service:
IN U.S.A.: P.O. Box 1341, Buffalo, NY 14240-8531
IN CANADA: P.O. Box 603, Fort Erie, Ontario L2A 5X3

Want to try 2 free books from another series! Call 1-800-873-8635 or visit www.ReaderService.com.

---

*Terms and prices subject to change without notice. Prices do not include sales taxes, which will be charged (if applicable) based on your state or country of residence. Canadian residents will be charged applicable taxes. Offer not valid in Quebec. This offer is limited to one order per household. Books received may not be as shown. Not valid for current subscribers to the Love Inspired or Love Inspired Suspense series. All orders subject to approval. Credit or debit balances in a customer's account(s) may be offset by any other outstanding balance owed by or to the customer. Please allow 4 to 6 weeks for delivery. Offer available while quantities last.

Your Privacy—Your information is being collected by Harlequin Enterprises ULC, operating as Harlequin Reader Service. For a complete summary of the information we collect, how we use this information and to whom it is disclosed, please visit our privacy notice located at corporate.harlequin.com/privacy-notice. From time to time we may also exchange your personal information with reputable third parties. If you wish to opt out of this sharing of your personal information, please visit readerservice.com/consumerschoice or call 1-800-873-8635. **Notice to California Residents**—Under California law, you have specific rights to control and access your data. For more information on these rights and how to exercise them, visit corporate.harlequin.com/california-privacy.

LIRLIS22R3

Get 4 FREE REWARDS!

We'll send you 2 FREE Books plus 2 FREE Mystery Gifts.

FREE
Value Over
$20

Both the **Harlequin® Special Edition** and **Harlequin® Heartwarming™** series feature compelling novels filled with stories of love and strength where the bonds of friendship, family and community unite.

YES! Please send me 2 FREE novels from the Harlequin Special Edition or Harlequin Heartwarming series and my 2 FREE gifts (gifts are worth about $10 retail). After receiving them, if I don't wish to receive any more books, I can return the shipping statement marked "cancel." If I don't cancel, I will receive 6 brand-new Harlequin Special Edition books every month and be billed just $5.49 each in the U.S. or $6.24 each in Canada, a savings of at least 12% off the cover price, or 4 brand-new Harlequin Heartwarming Larger-Print books every month and be billed just $6.24 each in the U.S. or $6.74 each in Canada, a savings of at least 19% off the cover price. It's quite a bargain! Shipping and handling is just 50¢ per book in the U.S. and $1.25 per book in Canada.* I understand that accepting the 2 free books and gifts places me under no obligation to buy anything. I can always return a shipment and cancel at any time by calling the number below. The free books and gifts are mine to keep no matter what I decide.

Choose one: ☐ **Harlequin Special Edition**
(235/335 HDN GRJV)

☐ **Harlequin Heartwarming**
Larger-Print
(161/361 HDN GRJV)

Name (please print)

Address   Apt. #

City   State/Province   Zip/Postal Code

Email: Please check this box ☐ if you would like to receive newsletters and promotional emails from Harlequin Enterprises ULC and its affiliates. You can unsubscribe anytime.

Mail to the **Harlequin Reader Service:**
IN U.S.A.: P.O. Box 1341, Buffalo, NY 14240-8531
IN CANADA: P.O. Box 603, Fort Erie, Ontario L2A 5X3

Want to try 2 free books from another series? Call 1-800-873-8635 or visit www.ReaderService.com.

---

*Terms and prices subject to change without notice. Prices do not include sales taxes, which will be charged (if applicable) based on your state or country of residence. Canadian residents will be charged applicable taxes. Offer not valid in Quebec. This offer is limited to one order per household. Books received may not be as shown. Not valid for current subscribers to the Harlequin Special Edition or Harlequin Heartwarming series. All orders subject to approval. Credit or debit balances in a customer's account(s) may be offset by any outstanding balance owed by or to the customer. Please allow 4 to 6 weeks for delivery. Offer available while quantities last.

Your Privacy—Your information is being collected by Harlequin Enterprises ULC, operating as Harlequin Reader Service. For a complete summary of the information we collect, how we use this information and to whom it is disclosed, please visit our privacy notice located at corporate.harlequin.com/privacy-notice. From time to time we may also exchange your personal information with reputable third parties. If you wish to opt out of this sharing of your personal information, please visit readerservice.com/consumerschoice or call 1-800-873-8635. **Notice to California Residents**—Under California law, you have specific rights to control and access your data. For more information on these rights and how to exercise them, visit corporate.harlequin.com/california-privacy.

HSEHW22R3

COUNTRY LEGACY COLLECTION

19 FREE BOOKS IN ALL!

Cowboys, adventure and romance await you in this new collection! Enjoy superb reading all year long with books by bestselling authors like Diana Palmer, Sasha Summers and Marie Ferrarella!